VALLEY OF FOOLS

BRIAN MARTELL

Copyright © 2020 by Brian Martell

All rights reserved. This book or any portion thereof may not be reproduced or transmitted in any form or manner, electronic or mechanical, including photocopying, recording, or by any information storage or retrieval system, without the express written permission of the copyright owner except for the use of brief quotations in a book review or other noncommercial uses permitted by copyright law.

Printed in the United States of America

LCCN: 2020918791
ISBN: Softcover 978-1-64908-373-9
eBook 978-1-64908-372-2
Republished by: PageTurner Press and Media LLC
Publication Date: 9/23/2020

To order copies of this book, contact:

PageTurner Press and Media
Phone: 1-888-447-9651
order@pageturner.us
www.pageturner.us

I've got to write this in order to get out of here. I'm in a home for depressed morons and crazy bastards. Mandatory commitment for conspiracy to murder. I'm innocent, but that doesn't matter.

I was institutionalized when I was sixteen for almost killing my next door neighbor. His name was Lyle Caldoff, and I blew up his car with a can of gasoline and some rags. The reason I blew up his car was because Lyle set my Uncle Vernon's cat, Josi, on fire with some gasoline and stood there laughing while she ran around the yard screaming. She didn't die right away. Josi was a year older than me. Uncle Vernon was about a hundred years older than both of us and real fond of that cat. I guess losing Josi broke his heart, because he had a stroke a week after she died. It'd been just the three of us for so long that everything just kind of fell apart then. I was going to have to move in with some complete strangers because I was too young to be on my own. I was mad, but mostly upset; I blew up Lyle's car, but I swear I didn't know he was sleeping off a hangover in the back seat. He was burnt some, pretty bad on his legs and buttocks, and someone said I was laughing while Lyle rolled around in the street with his pants on fire. I don't remember. I was surprised as hell Lyle was even in the car.

I was only supposed to be institutionalized until I turned eighteen, but some wires got crossed. A counselor in the juvenile system argued to the Judge that I was a danger to society, so I ended up at Heartsfield instead. The reason I was considered a danger was because the counselor, a guy named Eric Whitebird, wanted me to write a letter of apology to Lyle and his parents for blowing up their car, and I told Eric to shove the letter up his Native American ass. I wanted a letter of apology from Lyle first. Eric said I was being immature, since Josi was just a cat. Then I threatened to set him on fire, just to show him what it was like, only I didn't realize he had a tape recorder going. Eric played the tape at my release hearing, and the Judge acted like I was serious about it. Then I really blew it. I was only eighteen, and I called the Judge a fucking idiot. He acted like I'd insulted God. Judge Marshal. Fat old Judge Marshal. He's dead now, too. And Eric Whitebird is a fat ass DA in Wisconsin. I heard he was running for Judge up in Polk County. Hope I never have to sit in front of him for anything. He and Judge Marshal thought they were Gods, I swear. What a couple of Bozos.

After my catastrophic court appearance, I was committed to Heartsfield Home. I was eighteen years old and an idiot. And if you're trying to tell me you weren't an idiot at age eighteen, then you still are. I'm not going to argue with you.

The thing was, I understood the importance of having principles. I did not understand the principles themselves, but I respected the fact that I should have some. A man without principles is no better than a dog.

My principle, at age 18, was fairness. The fact that I had to apologize to Lyle, and he didn't have to apologize to me, struck me as grossly unfair. I could not respect a system that failed to recognize that blatant disregard for fairness. Heartsfield's not like what you'd expect if you watch much tv. There aren't lunatics shuffling down the hall, slobbering and clutching at your clothes. Mr Pensky might approach you, timidly hold up his game board and ask you to help find his checkers, but he isn't insistent about it. Hank, the big Japanese kid, may startle you by suddenly leaping up from the couch and chasing down a stray fly buzzing around the recreation room, but there's nothing to be frightened of. Especially after you've been there awhile and get to know everyone's quirks.

Actually, boredom's the most dangerous thing about a place like Heartsfield. Boredom seems like nothing, but it creeps up on you. Eventually, the skull thickens and traps thoughts inside and after awhile they begin to buzz, resonating apathy that blurs out everything else. At Heartsfield, I've seen guys come in wild-eyed desperate, skin and bones and on the edge of something, an idea, riding one big wave so high and long they're burning wild with adrenaline, oozing the stuff so it drips off their fingers like flaming kerosene: scorches the tile where they pace up and down the hallway, muttering prophecies. But after a few months of the Mexican kid's mashed potatoes and meatloaf and a soft bed, clean sheets and hot showers, they settle down and soften up, and before too long they're just a blob of softness and boredom and they get sent back out into the streets to get sliced apart. Them guys never come back, because they've seen what the system can do to you, and once you've been broke like that, it shakes your confidence. Most guys end up joining the system, once they see how it works. The rest just seem to give up altogether, seeking shelter in a resonating buzz of apathy.

The staff recognizes the danger of apathy. Once a guy has slipped beneath the surface, it's hard to bring him back up. Some guys get so apathetic they don't even want to brush their teeth or shower, and things can get pretty nasty. To help combat boredom, the staff devised a major theraputic tool: the committee.

Committees are a big deal around Heartsfield, designed to boost confidence. By voting with the majority, the majority gets what the majority wants, creating a general sense of self-satisfaction. Like it or not, self satisfaction is the basis of democracy. Or at least a democracy with undefined moral parameters.

Not that there are great moral debates being waged by Heartsfield's committees. Most of it is just trivial, everyday matters. Still, I'd like to think that common sense would prevail in regards to as simple a task as raking leaves, a contentious issue long debated by the first committee I ever joined: the Lawn Committee. The majority wanted to rake the leaves in the fall of the year, the traditional time to do so. And the proper time, if the trees have dropped their leaves. But any idiot could see that the oak trees growing on the Heartsfield property held onto their leaves through most of the damn winter, and it was just a waste of time to rake in the fall. Eventually the majority voted to rake twice a year, spring and fall, condescendingly agreeing with me, but not until after I'd quit in disgust.

By that time, I'd been at Heartsfield for about a year. That's usually when it starts to get to a guy. Boredom, I mean. Some guys go down sooner. Usually it's the prophets with the least endurance for institutional life. Old bums are more resilient, and some actually thrive without the bottle. But just about everyone has a mental marker on the time of year they were committed, and when the winter snows began to melt into my second spring at Heartsfield, the first signs of apathy began to appear.

Desperately bored, I began to rebel. I refused to join any more committees. Everyone is suppose to belong to a committee. It's part of the theraputic design. My refusal became my flag. I was young and strong. I didn't even know how strong I was. I'd never been tested. Lord, was I strong. I refused to cooperate. I became a fortress of resolve.

Various counselors worked patiently to pierce my resolve. But they were paid by the system, and I viewed them as part of a conspiracy against cultural dissent. With each attempt my resolve deepened, tempered with conviction. They tried to reason, but I'd learned to hate. I hated my situation. Hate acts as a catalyst, allowing anger to expand way beyond reason. I was unreasonable, I admit. But I thought I was trapped.

So I sat in the rec room everyday, smoking cigarettes and watching inane tv programs while the rest of the residents attended committee meetings. I realized the futility of my revolt, but I resolved to make one less pawn available for manipulation by a system governed by a majority of idiots. I began a long journey of conscientious withdrawal, and sank into the deep, stagnate waters of apathy.

Several years passed which I hate even to think about. Beneath the surface of apathy, I was miserable.

With clentched fists, I moved through the halls of Heartsfield, an angry martyr. Sensing my hate, for I hated my misery, people instinctively avoided me. Other than my roommate, Ron, who couldn't keep his mouth shut for more than three minutes without breaking a sweat, few people spoke to me while I responded with little more than a disinterested grunt.

After a few years, my behavior lost its novelty and was accepted as the norm by everyone at Heartsfield, including myself. I did nothing to dispel this image, and it wasn't because I didn't care. Being a menace became my shield: an impenetrable alloy of anger and hate. I was indestructable then. No one could reach me, and few tried.

At least I was impervious to exterior assaults. Inside I was tearing myself apart. I hate to give him too much credit, for I believe he's gotten more credit than he actually deserves, but sometimes I wonder what would have become of me if Ed Ludgrin hadn't been committed to Heartsfield four years after I was. He was unique. An original crazy bastard is sometimes considered a genius, although having spent a quarter of my life around them, I would insist that a crazy bastard is just that, regardless of what the average guy on the street might think about it. What made this guy's approach different was that he gained the system's approval; a very novel idea. In fact, he won a Pulitzer Prize for his volume of essays. Maybe you've heard of him. His name was Ed

Ludgrin, and he produced a volume of work titled 'Moments'.

Ed was a psychopath with a severely abbreviated attention span, having been committed to Heartsfield suffering from delusions of creativity and malnutrion. Creativity, to Ed, was anything unusual, or anything so usual that it had to be considered universal. Ed thought he had vision to discern such things and was always trying to point them out to everyone. A fly landing on a white wall would excite him, and he'd hold his hands up to his eyes to form something like a frame for the vision, elaborating to anyone bored enough to listen about how that fly had transformed the wall into something more than a wall by interacting with it to form a moment. 'Moments' were a big deal to Ed. He was always looking for them. He had a way of getting on your nerves, with his moments. That's why he ended up at Heartsfield. He was so taken by moments that his days had become so fragmented he was unable to take care of himself. He was damn near starving when he came in, his eyes hollow and sunk in his head beneath dark, bushy eyebrows. When he looked at you it was with an analytical eye, scrutinizing everything you did until you dropped something or tripped, and then he'd snap his hands up around his eyes, forming a frame and taking a mental picture.

Ed sort of hung around with me and Ron because nobody else liked him, he made everyone so nervous. Nobobdy liked Ron either, so he was just happy to have someone around to talk to. Ron hated to be alone more than anything. He used to follow me into the bathroom and talk to me through the stall door, even though I never said six words in a row back at him and whatever gave him the impression I was listening was always a mystery to me. Ed listened though, and he'd nod his head at something Ron was saying, something about a shop project Ron had built in high school, a bird feeder or something, and Ed would picture it, staring at the wall, sometimes holding his hands up to his eyes and tilting his head sideways as though to get a different perspective. They were a real pair, Ron and Ed.

The staff's goal with Ed was to teach him to string these moments together. To relate them, like a deck of cards with pictures on them that seem to move when you flip them fast and steady with your thumb. From still life to motion pictures. They attempted to achieve continuity in Ed by requiring him to keep a journal of his daily experiences. Apparently this idea of writing down moments appealed to Ed, for he immersed himself in his project, producing a volume of work that was submitted for publication by one of the nurses, and I'll be damned if Ed didn't win a Pulitzer. He was discharged with honors, his work being translated into five languages and distributed internationally. I read one of his reviews in TIME magazine where Ed was being credited with offering hope to the human race. So in the end, I guess Ed did prove himself to be a genius. But that doesn't mean he wasn't a crazy bastard. He was, more so than the average guy anyways.

Perhaps it's not obvious why I consider Ed to be such an important figure in my life. He really wasn't that important, but by beating the system, he gave me unexpected hope. I must admit a grudging admiration for the runt, for Ed was the same when he left Heartsfield as when he came in. They never broke him.

It wasn't necessary. Some people are miserable enough to take care of themselves.

Not long after Ed was discharged, another influential person entered my life. Angela Blackmore. Angela was a mature woman, about thirty-five, and had cool eyes. Very cool and controlled. I often caught her cool gaze as I sat on the couch, smoking, while everyone else was at the committee meetings. I thought she might be attracted to the rebel image. She wasn't.

Angela was the most recent in a series of previously anonymous staff administrators, whose purpose seemed vaguely benign. Consequently, I perceived her rather ambiguously. As a willing pawn of the system, her intelligence and willpower were suspect. On the other hand, she was damn pretty. The truth was, I had feelings for Angela.

Conditioned to concealing my feelings beneath a mask of indifference, I naively assumed this approach to familiarity to be widely understood and accepted. I read much more into her cool gaze, her curt greetings as we passed each other in the hallway, then she obviously intended. Attracted by her aloofness, I responded in kind.

That's why I was so surprised the morning Angela tapped my shoulder while I was standing in the lunch line.

"Mr Emerson," she said, very polite. All the Staff were very polite. I resented it. It sounded very condescending to me.

"Mr Emerson, would you please stop by my office this afternoon? There's a matter I would like to discuss with you. If two o'clock fits into your schedule, that would be fine with me."

I resented the insinuation that I would be busy at two o'clock. Angela knew as well as anybody that at two o'clock I would be sitting on the couch in the Rec Room smoking cigarettes and watching tv.

As much as I resented Angela's condescending attitude, I was looking forward to the meeting. Years of daytime talk shows had influenced my imagination. Possible scenarios ran through my mind, all sharing a similar conclusion.

At five minutes after two, I got up from the couch and sauntered down the hallway to Angela's office. With a cigarette dangling from my mouth, I knocked on the open door and leaned against the jamb, looking cool. She was at her desk, back to me, busily working and did little more than glance over her shoulder and order me to put the cigarette out and take a seat in the vacant chair just inside. There wasn't any place to put the cigarette so I dropped it on the floor and stepped on it. I both resented and admired Angela's attitude. After a minute of staring at Angela's back, I was about to get up and return to the couch when she finally wheeled around in her chair and took off her glasses. Another ten seconds and I'd been gone. Angela had a serious look on her face. It was easier to act bored when she wasn't looking so damn pretty, and I felt in control.

"Mr Emerson, we've got to talk."

I just shrugged my shoulders. She was about to try to reach me, and I was getting ready to thwart her every attempt.

"As administrator here at Heartsfield, I am faced with some very hard choices. You watch the news, Mr Emerson. Every day you watch tv. Surely you have heard of the budget problems facing the city?"

I was only half listening. There was a picture of a little girl smiling on Angela's desk. A little girl in a white dress, maybe two or three years old. She had the same cool eyes.

"The effects of the revenue shortfall are far reaching. There have been some reallocations of funds. Simply a shuffling of the cards, really. Accounting tricks. The mayor has chosen to finance a few high profile programs at the expense of less politically rewarding ones, such as the expansion of facilities like Heartsfield, which nobody wants in this neighborhood anyway. I'm afraid we're considered a liability to our new neighbors. Are you following what I'm saying, Mr Emerson?"

I just shrugged again. The little girl intrigued me. It could've been Angela at age three. The same cool eyes.

"There are regulations—quotas, if you will. In the past these quotas did not hold much sway, since the mental health system had been depleted of many residents during the social reintroduction mentality of the seventies and eighties. However, in recent years an increasing number of lawyers are relying on insanity pleas as a defense strategy. This has begun to strain the system. By law, I am required to provide 90 percent of our resources to accomodate these mandatory commitments. I've had to make choices—difficult choices. I've gone through your file, Mr Emerson, and I've witnessed your behavior here at Heartsfield. Let me begin by asking you a simple question: 'Are you happy here at Heartsfield?'"

It seemed like a stupid question. Some sort of trap. Approaching it carefully, I just shrugged and acted bored.

"It sucks," I answered.

Angela smiled. "I guess that was an obvious question. So let me follow it up with a less obvious one. Why do you continue to stay here at Heartsfield?" I was uneasy. I couldn't see where she was headed. I decided to play it safe.

She knew why I was there. I answered without telling her anything. "Judge Marshal ordered me here."

Angela looked concerned. "I know he did. I've gone through your file.

But why do you coninue to stay?"

The whole trick of being a menace is emotional equilibrium. Apathy. Don't give a damn about nothing. You can be hateful, but only if someone's trying to help you. By showing concern, Angela was signaling to me that something was wrong, meant to feed on my insecurities and wear down my resolve. Then she could come to my rescue. I knew the game well, and volleyed. "Judge Marshal ordered me here" I repeated.

"I know he did. I've gone through your file. Surely you are aware of the subsequent release hearing, requested by a Mr . . .," she picked my file from the clutter of her desk and flipped through it. It was a thick file, a manila folder stuffed with typed evaluations and handwritten notes. She pulled out a page and began reading from it. "A Mr Whitebird. It's all right here. On recommendation of Mr Whitebird, Judge Marshal converted your admission here from mandatory to voluntary less than a year later."

Dazed, I groped about for something to latch onto—a distraction; something to buy time. I needed to think. A ping-pong ball was bouncing down the hallway in diminishing intervals, slippers slapping on the linoleum in pursuit, then sliding into position for the scoop. Probably Hank. Maybe Ron. He caught it before it bounced past Angela's office, so I couldn't see who it was.

"Mr Emerson?"

"Why wasn't I made aware of the hearing results?" I demanded, trying to focus and cover up with anger. Voluntary? My mind was spinning. Footsteps fading up the hallway linoleum, and I'm going down. I don't know how far yet, but I'm going down.

"But you must have been. Here is a letter, a copy of a letter sent to you advising you of the hearing results, dated July 17, 1986. You signed the receipt form, verifying you received the letter. It's all right here in your file. And your files were available to you the entire time, so certainly you must have been aware of your voluntary status?"

She handed me my file, but my eyes wouldn't focus. It was my signature all right, but I'd never read the letter, I swear. Maybe I did. I was confused. It was my signature, but I don't ever remember reading the damn letter.

"Why?" I asked, but I didn't even know what I was asking about.

"On recommendation of Mr Whitebird," Angela took the file back and began paging through it. "He felt it was in your best interest to have a stable environment. It was a very troubled time for you, Mr Emerson. A hormonal imbalance, perhaps. Mr Whitebird felt that it would be best if you stayed here at Heartsfield until you felt ready to cope with the outside world. Judge Marshal agreed, on condition that your release be approved by the current staff administrator, which brings us to the present situation. You say you are unhappy here at Heartsfield, and I am under pressure to operate under a budget that does not allow room for expansion. I must make room for the increasing number of mandatory commitments."

A hormonal imbalance?

"Are you telling me that I've been free to leave this place for six years?" I tried to sound angry, but I must have been looking sick because Angela patted my arm and tried to reassure me.

"Please do not feel pressured into leaving, Mr Emerson. This has been your home for the last six years, and we don't want to make you feel unwelcome.

It is a big adjustment to leave the security of Heartsfield for the uncertainty of the outside world." She was jabbing me, stealing my breath; the menace in the corner trying to cover up. "But you are unhappy, and it would be in the best interest of everyone if you were to consider it. The state will supply you with a set of clothes and a room at one of the local motels, along with two hundred dollars to help you get started in your new life. The rent will be paid for eighteen months and a social worker will stop by and visit you during that time to help with the adjustment. Don't worry, Mr Emerson, we won't abandon you at this vulnerable time in your life."

I couldn't stand it. My mind was spinning. Menace, what a joke. Marshal and Whitebird had had the last laugh. Hormonal imbalance, for Christ's sake. "Now, if you will excuse me, I've a staff meeting in ten minutes, and I haven't prepared a single note. It's a hard time for everyone. I'm afraid there will be some long faces today, as I must reduce our staff, and Lord knows the people here are over worked as it is. Your release papers would normally be prepared in forty-eight hours, but due to the staff work load, it may take slightly longer. So take your time, Mr Emerson, don't feel rushed, but please give us plenty of notice when you do decide to leave us."

I got up from the chair and had to lean against the wall for support. Angela smiled and patted my arm again. I felt like an idiot and hated her for making me feel that way, even though I knew it wasn't her fault. Six years I'd been stalking around Heartsfield, making an ass of myself. I decided I had to get out now. There was nothing else to do but leave now.

I staggered back to the room and stripped off my greens. Since it was Tuesday the only set of street clothes I owned were in the laundry. My roommate, Ron, had a blue corduroy sports suit he said I could have, and a suitcase. Ron would give you anything. He was all right, he just wanted people to like him.

"You really leaving now?" he kept asking, fidgeting around like a kid and getting in the way. He actually thought I was a menace and that I was going to bust out of Heartsfield. I didn't tell him I was voluntary, like he was. Just to get him out of the way—he wanted to fold everything before stuffing the suitcase, I gave him a twenty, all the money I had, and sent him down to get cigarettes for me. I meant for him to get change and buy me a pack of smokes, but he was so excited he came back with an armful. He'd even pitched in a couple bucks of his own. Ron was all right, just a nervous kid. I didn't call him an idiot for spending my savings on cigarettes, but instead I thanked him and promised to write.

With the suitcase in hand and Ron bouncing excitedly beside me, I marched down the hallway toward the front entrance, right past the staff meeting room, where Angela was giving someone the ax. She heard me yelling, and the entire staff emptied out into the hallway to see what was going on.

"Unlock the door," I was yelling, "Unlock the door or I'll kick it down." The poor guy on duty at the front desk looked scared and confused and wouldn't get out of the way. Ron was excited and kept warning the guy that I was a menace and he better do what I said. There were a lot of people gathering around asking questions and I kept warning the guy to unlock the door when suddenly Angela spoke, very cool and in control.

"Mr Emerson," she said, and everyone got quiet to hear what she was going to say. "I would advise you to wait until proper arrangements can be made to assist your adjustment to the outside world. There are no free meals out there, you know."

"He knows that." Ron was excited as hell. "Better unlock the door, or he's going to kick it down."

An excited buzz went through the crowd and everyone wanted to see if this guy was really as bad as he'd put on for the last six years. And I was so mad, I felt like kicking something. Then Angela shot me down again.

"If you insist on leaving, then, you will find that the door is not locked.

Good luck, mr. Emerson."

She looked at me so cool and bored I almost got scared and went back to the room, but it was too late. The door wasn't locked, and Ron was telling me to write, and I was out in the cold rain with a suitcase full of undearwear and cigarettes and less than a dollar's worth of change in my pocket.

The intensity burned and sizzled like a whip slicing through the air and I flinched, cowering from the snap of light that seized the world, and the roar of angry thunder which brutally shook it free. Rain fell with such force it shattered against the earth, forming a haze that hovered over the pavement. The door clicked shut behind me. A brief but intense internal debate commenced, the line drawn between panic and pride. Angela would let me back in. All I had to do was ask.

I stared down into the valley as I'd done countless times before. The scene below was both familiar and unknown. I'd been above it all, looking down on it for six years—the dirty brick buildings and the dark, narrow back alleys; rush hour traffic, the flashing neon, and the fog. Headlights glowed dull yellow in the mist, crossing the Brewery Street Bridge. It was early for headlights, but the clouds hung low and heavy, especially down in the valley. Some mornings the whole valley was lost in clouds, just the brewery smokestacks poking up through. You can't even see the bridge on mornings like that, not until the sun climbed high enough to reach down to the river. Then, slowly, the fog would lift, rising on the updrafts like a curtain lifting on a stage set. It was a secure point of veiw. Heartsfield was a safe observation post. Solid, with its ivy covered brick, massive steps and imposing doors. Heavy and tight. Solid and safe.

I tried collecting my thoughts, but they were so scattered it was confusing. The lawn was a mess, a mat of brown leaves smoldering thick and wet. It should have been raked three weeks ago. Squirrels rummaged for last fall's acorns, burrowing in the leaves and chasing over-head along the twisted black branches of the ancient oaks. I could no more organize my thoughts than herd the squirrels into a little circle on the ground, lecturing them on the need for cohesiveness and cooperation for the common good of all squirrels. It'd be difficult, but maybe not impossible, especially if I had a sack of corn and enough time to tame them all.

Forget the damn squirrels, Emerson. Organize.

I tried to think, but the squirrels were distracting as hell. Chattering, its tail twitching, an albino squirrel came down the trunk of one of the big oaks head first and began plowing through the leaves, nose down, crossing the yard until it located an old acorn. With the acorn in its mouth, the white squirrel climbed up another tree and perched in the crotch of a lower branch, nibbling greedily and dropping crumbs on its belly.

White squirrels are a big deal in the Heartsfield neighborhood. Albinos. They're suppose to be rare, but for some reason they're almost as common as the grey ones around Heartsfield. There's even a bed and breakfast named after them, The White Squirrel Inn, just up the street. It's an old Victorian mansion built by a turn of the century lumber baron. It was a delapitated old boarding house when I'd first been committed. Peeling paint and sagging front porch, weeds growing a foot high in the rain gutters. The whole neighborhood was like that—huge mansions sagging under the weight of neglect. Rusting twenty year old chevys dripping oil, old refridgerators out back; over-worked waitresses, stoned prophets, punks, and late night police raids. Heartsfield itself was a massive brick building originally built as a private school for the local rich kids, but sold to the city after the neighborhood went to hell. Which was fine at the time when nobody gave a damn.

It was kind of a renaissance period for the neighborhood now, though. With their hardwood floors and soaring dormers, the old mansions were hot property on the local real estate market. One after the other they'd been converted to bed and breakfasts, changing the whole feel of the neighborhood. People who used to live around here would now be considered undesirable. You can get fifty dollars for a full set of Cadillac hubcaps, and during the transition period it was a real problem. Nobody from Heartsfield ever stole a hubcap, but resentment toward the residents ran high. Like an embarrassing cousin outrageously drunk at a formal wedding ceremony—obnoxious, but somewhat amusing. Tolerable, until he got sick on the floor during the dollar dance.

I was getting soaked standing on the front steps of Heartsfield, feeling torn and hesitant. It's hard to think clearly when you're freezing your ass off. Corduroy soaks up water like you wouldn't believe. The door was locked. I tried once, soft and easy just to see, but it was locked tight. I couldn't bring myself to knock, almost did once, then caught myself and lit another smoke, trying not to shake, but the wind blew right through the cheap suit and I was shaking whether I wanted to or not.

I could say I forgot something, go back to my room and hide under the covers for a day or so until one of the counselors came in and convinced me I had nothing to be ashamed of.

I almost knocked again and then, with a spasmodic jerk, I did. My knuckles struck the door and it immediately opened. A wave of warm, dry air drifted out like the glow off a fire, soaking through my wet clothing. Angela smiled good-naturedly, as though she were expecting me.

"Yes, Mr Emerson?"

She was so cool. And the guy at the front desk was under orders to ignore the situation so as not to embarrass me, pretending to be reading the newspaper, but the look of amusement on his face gave him away. I couldn't stand it. I couldn't go in. There was no way. Menace, what a joke. Angela waited, holding the door open but firmly blocking the way, self-assured in her expectations of me. Suddenly, I didn't care about it. About freezing to death, I mean.

"Just wanted to say good-bye."

For a brief second, Angela showed surprise, then concern, then nothing but self-assured coolness. I was down the steps before she answered.

"Mr Emerson?"

Her voice stopped me cold. "Yeah?'

"If you're about to impress the world, you may want to consider zipping up your fly, first."

The Bitch. The bitch. The bitch. Jesus, what a bitch. Man, I should have left years ago.

It was Tuesday, because Tuesdays are garbage days, and the trash cans were still on the sidewalk. I attacked the first clump of cans I came to. They belonged to the River Bluff Bed and Breakfast, a huge castle-like Victorian mansion with white columns and a cupola high atop the soaring roof, painted grey and white with intricate strokes of maroon detailing. The trash cans huddled innocently beside the wrought iron gate of the newly paved driveway; dented up galvanized cans just like everyone else's. Smoldering in the grey, cold rain, fingering the eighty cents in my pocket, I suddenly kicked a can. It went rattling down the steep sidewalk, the cover shaking loose and rolling free like a bicycle wheel out ahead. I kicked another. And then another and anotherandanother, and the cans were rattling loud and someone yelled "Hey!" and one of the cans bounced out into the street and 'whump,' disappeared beneath an MTC bus geared low and roaring loud. Faces in every window stared at me with curiosity as the bus engine choked and lurched to a jolting stop. The doors folded open and the Chinese bus driver leaned out, cursing me.

"You dumb son of a bitch, what the hell is your problem?"

I ignored him, pretending to be deaf, shrugging apathetically and continuing down the sidewalk as though it were my God-given right to kick trash cans anytime I felt like it.

The battered trash cans. Silver margarine foils scattered on the concrete, stuck wet and tight. Rainwater rippling in the gutter, swirling brown leaves and cigarette butts that hesitate, then disappear down the storm grates. Cars hissing up the street, spray rolling misty on the gusting wind.

Moments after my release from Heartsfield, I was growing increasingly concerned about the possibility of suffering a nervous collapse.

Grey. The clouds rolled low, thunder rumbling back over the bluffs. Big raindrops shot diagonally across the headlights, cold streams down my back and water squishing out my shoes with every step. Downhill I went.

From the mansions of the Heartsfield neighborhood, Brewery Street led down into a smoldering, twenty block area of dying commerce and crumbling brick buildings. Into the valley. The same valley they'd hauled Ed Ludgrin up from three years ago. Ed spoke of the valley often, declaring it a 'moment.' A drop of rain swelling at the tip of a dark twig, gathering, stretching, pausing to collect itself. One moment away from the fall. I'd listened wistfully and it's ironic, but the first place I was going to go after breaking free of Heartsfield was the Valley. I was going to start an uprising or something.

Onion grease and the electric buzz of neon. The valley was horns, music, roaring diesel busses, exhaust and tobacco. 'Jesus Saves' spray painted on the plywood covering half a block of storefront windows. Hecticity. Couldn't turn around without messing someone up; lights changing and people are moving **now**, bumping and jiving. Greased with familiarity and smooth because of it. Ambivalence. A phony kind of ambivalence in a way. The valley was a damn community. You could tell that right off. As much a moment as any, I guess, but snapping with life and understated cohesiveness.

It was strange, after so many years of waxed floors and florescent lights, to be standing in front of Stacey's Bar, on the corner of Brewery Street and Second, the sidewalk gritty under my feet. Horns honked as pedestrians dodged traffic with umbrellas lowered like battering rams against the wind. Swirling scraps of paper danced with the exhaust of the idling cars, the cold rain competing with the windshield wipers that swept methodically back and forth, the only sense of order and discipline in the whole scene.

A canopy over the sidewalk offered some shelter from the rain. A couple of guys were leaning in the open doorway, but when it became obvious I was going to hang around, they flicked their smokes out into the street and drifted back into the bar, Hound Dog Taylor bouncing off the walls and the sound of a cue ball ricocheting across a crowded table was followed by a loud obscenity and a burst of derisive laughter.

While the Brewery anchored the district, Stacey's was its harbor. It was a respectable bar, with two pool tables, a cigarette machine, and a jukebox. The jukebox leaned blue, thanks to Al the bartender's preference for reflective, straight-beat, beer sliding music. People went there to get drunk, laugh and lie and argue, and once or twice a week there was a fist fight of some kind. Knives were not allowed. If a man pulled a knife, one of two things happened. If he was lucky, someone grabbed him from behind and the rest of the bar proceeded to disarm him, beat him senseless, and throw him out back by the dumpster, providing a chance for serious reflection and possibly conversion. If he was unlucky, Al shot him. Word had gotten around, and the fights in Stacey's were old fashioned, steam blowing nose breakers—generally harmless affairs.

My impending nervous collapse worried the hell out of me, only this train of thought simply increased my anxiety level until I began to shake. The corduroy suit, in addition to looking stupid, was of absolutely no value as far as conserving body heat was concerned. There was a raincoat in my suitcase, but there was no way to open it with all the people walking around.

There wasn't any place to lay it down flat. I could've tried just opening it a little, standing up, but my socks and underwear would fall out the sides, and I wouldn't be able to close it again.

A flickering Budweiser sign in Stacey's window caught my eye. A bright pink neon sign, only the 'B' is burned out cold dead, so it says 'udweiser' instead. It was depressing. Someone's been plugging that sign in every morning for the last six years and they don't give a damn if the 'B' is burned out, and neither does anybody else, just plug the damn thing in, dump some ice in the urinal and turn on the soaps. It's just another crappy day, let's get it over with. On the smoky glass of the window, my reflection stared back at me. It was strange to see myself. Pathetic, really. Soaking wet, all hunched up and confused looking. Menace, what a joke. Just an idiot. I began to berate myself, chastizing my own reflection, staring with disgust and wilting further beneath my own scorn. Disdainfully, I sneered. Mockingly, taunting, sensing my own vulnerablity and attacking ruthlessly as the sounds of the street faded away. "But why do you continue to stay, that is my question? (Are you afraid to leave?)"

"Surely you must have known?"

What else had I missed in six years? What other bits of fundamental truths had been staring me in the face, obscured by my own self-centered sense of reality?

Gradually, the sound of laughter began to infiltrate my consciousness. Derisive laughter. The jukebox was quiet, the laughter filled the void and a warm wave of embarrassment washed over me as this squinty looking guy wearing a dirty white bartender's apron stepped out of the open doorway, a bushy handle-bar mustache drooping over his mouth. He was wiping his hands on the apron, looking at me like I was stark naked.

"You got some sort of problem, buddy?"

My eyes focused beyond my reflection, past the udweiser sign, into the bar where half a dozen guys were leaning on cue sticks, bent over with laughter and making faces back at me. One guy dropped his pants, his hairy ass mooning right out at me. I immediately assumed a bored expression, mostly just reflexes. Al started looking mean.

"If I were you, friend, I'd just keep walking," and he's still wiping his hands, only real slow now.

"Watch out, Al, he looks dangerous," someone yelled from inside the bar, laughter rolling out behind it. Embarassing as hell. I took Al's advice. The whole damn world belonged to Al and his buddies right then, laughing at the geek in the window.

I need a plan.

Half a dozen pigeons flapped overhead, grey and white, stalling on the wind, swerving up and then down hard on a heavy gust, sweeping wide and gliding fast and smooth back down toward the river. Traffic was all fouled up. Horns were honking and the lights were red, and I froze in panic halfway across the intersection. Tires spun on the wet pavement and a young, blonde haired woman behind the wheel of a red sports car flipped me the bird, mouthing obscenities through the glass as though she hated my guts and wanted to hit me. The yellow line offered refuge from physical trauma, if not verbal abuse, and I stood there until the lights changed in my favor, ignoring the stares and gestures as though my purpose far outweighed any inconvenience my presence created.

My vision became shortsighted and for a moment continuity was lost. The mist off the tires swirled on a gust, cold steam and fog. Brake lights glowed bright, shining on the wet pavement and umbrellas, red and blue like huge flowers, began blooming thick all around me. One after the other the umbrellas bloomed, the sidewalk crowded to a halt, and I became wedged in a mass of bodies. Exactly what the crowd stood for mattered little. I joined with gratitude, overjoyed that they ignored me. To be ignored was akin to being accepted. The warmth of their bodies brought relief from the wind and had a comforting, stabilizing effect. Cough drops and perfume. Tobacco and hair spray, coffee and perspiration mingled on the rising waves of body heat, soothing the raw nerves of my soul, and I became one of many.

Someone shoved a bright red 'Mckinnley for Senate' button in my hand. It was a political rally for the mayor. He stood above the crowd, up on the concrete steps of the Brewery, smiling humbly and waving friendly, flanked by several bodyguards in dark suits and shaded glasses, one of whom held an umbrella to protect the mayor's hair from the rain. Despite my grudge towards the system represented by Mayor Mckinnley, I greeted him with applause. It was his crowd. They had adopted me, and I wanted their approval. Still, a mild pang of discomfort ran contrary to the flow of goodwill I was experiencing. It was the mayor's hair. Even in the wind his silver hair sat poised. Alert hair, tense and coiled tight, as though trying to avoid detection by remaining perfectly still. I'm irrational around tense hair, with an innate sense of distrust that has its roots deep in my subconscious. Judge Marshal had hair like that, but his hair had made me nervous, too, so it goes back further than that. I don't know. I wish I'd never even thought about it. I squinted to put his hair out of focus, trying to forget about it, clapping louder, nodding and smiling at the folks around me whenever they did. The speech was going over well. The mayor was a Democrat, so naturally he was blaming the Republicans for the mess. That always cracks me up. Nobody wants to blame people for being greedy and lazy; they always blame Democrats or Republicans, depending on which side they're on.

"Do the Republicans care about the plight of the homeless, those misfortunate souls among us who live lives of desperation while they discuss mutual funds, poolside, reaping the bounty of the working man while dismissing the plight of displaced workers? For remember, friends, there but for the grace of God Himself, or Herself, for that matter, go I. What-so-ever you do to the least of my brothers, or sisters, that you do unto me. The bottom line, friends, is that what goes around, comes around. Let a wound fester and gangrene may set in. I suggest my Republican colleages take notice of the festering wound, lest their privileged lifestyle suffer the fate of every elitist class in the history of mankind, or womankind, which failed to monitor its own greed. Adequate dental care for all. That is my proposal. It is a simple proposal. A simple start. But it is a start, and that is important. Because there is a need to begin, friends, for the wound festers."

Then he went on talking about blood poisoning and failing health. It all made sense, in a way, but he was dragging it out quite a bit. Several of the local tv stations had crews on hand, and I recognized Roxanne Hendley, the On-The-Scene-Reporter for channel three. Roxanne was a stunning brunette who enuciated well, seemingly destined to anchor her own newscast some day. It was kind of exciting to see her in person. Roxanne was something of a local star, appearing nightly at tragic scenes all over the city, interviewing distraught family members and exhausted fire chiefs.

"Mr. Mayor," Roxanne shouted, "there is an opinion held by some that your dental care proposal is simply a campaign gimmick. That it is simply too expensive for these times of soaring deficits and revenue shortfalls. How would you respond to such an opinion, sir?"

The mayor leaned forward from beneath the umbrella, trying to catch Roxanne's question over the street noise. It was sad to see his bodyguard, a big serious looking guy, getting soaked while holding an umbrella over the mayor's hair. The mayor didn't even seem to notice him there, he's just leaning out at Roxanne, and when he caught the question he sort of sagged, running a hand across his face in tired frustration.

"Ms. Hendley," (Roxanne beams at the mention of her name.) "you ever have an abscessed tooth? It's a bad pain. Feels like a sixteen penny nail slammed straight down through to the nerve. You can't deny it. Kind of pain that drives a man crazy, sweating in a ninety-five degree efficiency at two in the morning, pacing the room like a trapped animal desperate for release. Any release. And no-one's going to help you unless you have the money. Or beg. Cost him two weeks take-home pay to fix it if he were able to save it on nine dollars an hour. Man shouldn't have to beg for relief from an abscessed tooth. The country's broke, but the corporations are rich. There are vast sums of wealth. Record profits. Obscene salaries. Where'd they get the money? From us, dammit. We are the country. All I'm asking for is a voluntary contribution from those who can afford it. With public disclosure, both coming and going. Track the money. Put it on the internet and let the weirdos analyze it. It's not unreasonable. If you don't want to help, don't. But society is going to pay the price if someone doesn't. Sure I want to get elected. I want to shake the tree. Why the hell else would I be doing this?"

A round of applause went up from the crowd and the mayor descended the steps on a triumphant note, wading in and shaking hands. The crowd surged, catching me off guard and shoving me forward. A solid mass of bodies pressed closer and pinned me in tight and suddenly my nerves began to act up. 'Sen-a-tor Mc-kinn-ley, Sen-a-tor Mc-kinn-ley', the crowd began to chant, growing increasingly rambunctious. I began to panic, everything blown out of proportion. It was his hair. I became phobic toward the mayor's hair. It seemed to crouch on his head, steathily alert, like a wolverine, waiting patiently as the mayor, smiling naively, carried it deeper into the crowd. "Sen-a-tor Mc-kinn- ley, Sen-a-tor Mc-kinn-ley'

The crowd pushed ahead, and suddenly my mind reeled. A maroon wave lifted and carried me backwards, caught in the throes of an anxiety attack. Blindly backing away, frantically tugging at my suitcase, I struggled to break free of the crowd. Faces blurred, someone cursed and suddenly there was daylight ahead. I lunged forward, breaking free of the mob and crumbling to my knees, trying to catch my breath, unable to stop shaking.

"You got some sort of problem, buddy?"

A pair of black, polished shoes were planted on the sidewalk in front of me. Dark blue pants and a dark suitcoat and dark, shaded glasses. The mayor's bodyguard maintained a somber disposition; his manner of speaking did not suggest concern. Instinctively, I assumed a bored expression and got up, rolling my head back to meet his gaze. On the surface of his glasses my reflection stared back. It was pathetic. Soaking wet, shaking, a blank stare on my face which seemed to indicate a low level of cerebral activity. I flinched, and he smiled.

"Now, I think it'd be best if you just keep on walking, buddy."

There was nothing to do but take his advice, too. In need of shelter, behaving irrationally, destitute and confused—in my condition, I could've easily been mistaken for a crazy bastard, and probably hauled in; back into the system. Panic rose in my throat, and I almost broke into a run, but instead I managed to act bored and slowly turned away from the son of a bitch, trying to organize my thoughts. Behind me the crowd chanted.

'Sen-a-tor Mc-kinn-ley, Sen-a-tor Mc-kinn-ley' I needed a plan.

There was a bus shelter just up the street. Inside it smelled like stale cigarettes, butts scattered on the wet concrete along with a newspaper plastered wet and tight. The pages were all bled together, but the headlines were decipherable: "Mckinnley Steps Up Bid For Senate." Below, there was a picture of the mayor smiling and shaking someone's hand.

The plastic bench was empty except for an old guy at one end and at the other sat a young gal with two little girls in ponytails; yellow and pink ribbons and little fuzzy ponytails all over their heads. No one objected when I sat down with my suitcase. The little girls stared at my socks and greens and cigarettes, but no one said anything except the old guy is mumbling but it's not about anything I've ever done.

My raincoat wasn't in the suitcase. Ron said I could have it, but I must've forgotten to pack it. The wind swirled through and made a wet sound against the shelter plastic. I was shaking again, trying to get the suitcase shut.

"Your underwear's sticking out the side," one of the little girls said and the two of them started giggling and their mom warned them to hush up. I smiled, but she wouldn't look at me. She'd seen the greens and pulled her girls to the far side of the bench, sheltering them with her body. They kept sneaking looks at me, scared now.

A diesel roared and water splashed up on the curb and a big red metro bus pulled up in front of the shelter. Bored faces in every window, grey and brown. Below, on the side of the bus, was a green pasture in which sat a young couple laughing over a cup of yogurt, a horse running through the sunshine. Only the whole scene was crusted white and splattered with brown road grime and black diesel soot. Depressing as hell.

The young mother pulled her girls off the bench, and they're looking back as she dragged them into the bus and the old guy tried to get up, but he's stiff and jerked and almost fell when I tried to help him. He looked at me with a threat, but it was mostly fear, and the bus driver looked at me with suspicion. I started fumbling with the suitcase, but it wouldn't shut and there was no place to go anyways. The driver yelled something but the diesel drowned it, and I just shrugged my shoulders. He shook his head in disgust and closed the door, pulling back out into traffic, tires hissing on the wet pavement.

I felt awkward, like a new Admission sitting in a far corner of the rec room paging through the old **People** magazines as though they were interesting, afraid to make an ass of myself by doing something stupid. My confidence was shot. It lay on the tile floor of Angela Blackmore's office; a twisted, charred, smoldering heap of lies. It was an uncomfortable feeling. Confidence is feeling comfortable in a situation. I was uncomfortable as hell. The suit was partly to blame. It looked stupid for one thing, and it was too small. They fed us damn good at Heartsfield. I hadn't missed a meal in six years. The suit was wet and tight and irritating and the bench was hard, cold plastic and I was fidgeting around, adjusting things, trying to get comfortable, when it occurred to me my wallet was missing. Somebody in the rally had picked my pocket.

It was disgusting. Not that there was anything of value in my wallet. Just an expired driver's license I'd gotten before being committed, and a rubber I'd never had the chance to use. I'd bought it on the annual field trip to the Science Museum. There was a dispenser on the wall of the men's room near the mineral exhibits. I bought it just in case. I didn't know when I'd meet a woman who'd let me try it out, but it seemed important that I should have one with me at all times in the event the opportunity should suddenly arise. It wasn't the fact that I was no longer prepared that bothered me so much. I'd been carrying it for two years and had never even approached coming close to an opportunity. In my present condition, the possibility seemed even more remote. What disgusted me was that someone would take advantage of a rally like that—the gathering of people, uniting for a common cause, (albeit, the Mayor's) but none the less sharing a kind of bond. And in the middle of it some bastard is sneaking around picking their pockets. A real bastard, whoever it was.

I just sat there, awkward and disgusted, watching the traffic, starting to feel detached. The rush of cars racing the traffic lights, pedestrians dodging across the street, the hiss of tires, sprays of mist; cold and grey and without a shred of familiarity to comfort me. It was getting dark, but at least the rain had thinned out. Just a mist now which formed halos around the street lights. Drops trickled down the shelter plastic, and I crawled inside a moment, declaring it mine and finding solace within. Slowly, at first, a drop would move, pause, then inch downward, joining another and then another and another and anotherandanotherandanother till it streamed with momentum, racing down the wall.

I had my hands framed around my eyes, watching the drops, when a briefcase carrying woman dressed sharp in executive blues wisked into the bus shelter. Without thinking, I pivoted around and looked at her through my hands. She shook her head, tightly crossing her legs and lighting a cigarette.

"This is the last damn time I take the bus," she said.

"I know a guy who won a Pulitzer Prize doing that." I tried to explain. "Doing what, may I ask?"

"Looking at the world frame by frame. He was a genius."

"Oh," she said, blowing smoke and hugging her elbows in tight, scrutinizing the passing traffic as though she had something on her mind. She was damn pretty—dark curly hair and kind of a healthy, brisk way about her. We just sat there sharing the bench, not ten feet apart, but the silence began to grow between us. I couldn't think of anything else to say. I racked my brain trying to come up with something. The fact that my wallet had been stolen didn't even matter. I just wanted to talk to her. For practice, if nothing else. The only women I was ever around before were nurses and staff personnel, kind of a professional relationship. But here was a woman in a spontaneous, casual setting, and I couldn't think of a damn thing to say. It was getting awkward. The silence hung heavy, growing thicker. I had to say something pretty quick. She was probably expecting me to, disappointed and maybe even insulted.

"What's your name?" I finally blurted out.

"Taxi!" she yelled, leaping from the bench and waving down a yellow cab pulling up to the traffic lights. She was damn pretty.

I just sat on the bench watching the raindrops trickle down the shelter plastic. Who'd ever thought that skinny little runt would've ever won a Pulitzer? He'd been living in a sewer tunnel before being committed to Heartsfield for crying out loud. He had a camp down by the river, cooking fish on an open fire and raiding dumpsters in the Brewery district to supplement his diet. That's how he was committed. He was sitting in a dumpster, studying the collage of garbage, and the flies interacting with it, when someone tossed in a case of Leiny bottles, cracking him on the head and knocking him out cold. Luckily, an alert trash collector spotted him rolling out with the garbage and called the cops. The rest is history.

Thinking about Ed, I started thinking about his camp down by the river. He'd described sections of abandoned sewer tunnel down below the bluffs about a quarter mile south of the bridge, hidden somewhere in the brush behind the sewer treatment plant. If the sections of drainage pipe were still down there it'd be a good place to hole up for the night. There wasn't anyplace else to go, and just the thought of looking for Ed's camp lifted my spirit. I had a plan, and left the bus shelter with a glimmer of hope.

The street was crowded with hardhats. In groups of twos and threes, with lunch boxes and yellow hardhats, the third shift brewery workers were arriving to punch in. A fraternity of yellow hardhats, laughing and swearing, nodding their heads in greeting and deferment as they climbed the concrete steps of the brewery, which meant it was almost eleven o'clock. Which meant absolutely nothing to me, for I was expected nowhere at anytime. Adrift. It's strange, being adrift. It's a combination of freedom and nothing. It's pointless, but then, that's the point.

Behind the brewery was a large parking lot crowded with cars and washed in white light. The bright lights pushed the darkness back, which could be seen crouching on the eastern edge beneath the trees and concentrated down in the ravines of the riverbank. Light filtered through the tree branches just enough to illuminate a small park adjacent to the car lot, near the head of the bridge. Just a couple of benches perched on the crest of the bluff. I paused, allowing my eyes time to adjust. The tree branch shadows danced with the passing headlights. The darkness of the ravines was profound.

There is a correlation between the brightness of light and the depths which defy it. They define and contradict each other. Light tempers darkness, hardens and deepens it. The shadows which remain in the city are hard and deep. But not necessarily evil. There is good in the darkness, and for this I am glad. Otherwise, I'd'a been dead meat.

The river bottom is a reality all its own, separated from the city by forty foot bluffs which drop off sudden and steep. In some places the bluffs are sheer walls of bare limestone, and in other places the ravines slice through the soft rock, cutting down sharp into little streams and swamps. From above the shadows deep in the ravines seemed pitch black and impenetrable. But once I slid down the ditch and made it to the bottom, my eyes adjusted and it was possible to look around. It was too dark to read a watch, but light enough to see the tree trunks.

The trees deepest in the ravines were huge. They had to be a hundred years old. Maybe more. It'd take three people to reach around some of them. Their bark was wrinkled deep and rough. I had to run my hands over them, not trusting my eyes in the dim light. They were the biggest God damn trees I've ever seen, outside of pictures. Cottenwoods. When a breeze blew down through the valley, their leaves flickered like rain. The seed is less than the size of a valium tablet, and it's hard to believe they could grow to such proportions. From the deepest shadows of the ravines the massive trunks rise up, dividing into three, four stems, towering over the whole ditch, until the top-most branches reach into the light filtering through off the city streets above. Some of them would've taken four guys with long arms to reach around.

The ravines were slick, wet with leaves, and it was difficult, with the suitcase, to climb up the ridges. The ridges offered some spectacular views of the valley, and I paused to rest and have a smoke. To the north, traffic rolled across the Brewery Street Bridge, yellow headlights stretching high over the river. To the east, the bluffs were dark; a sheer mass of blackness defined by the lights of the city which glowed at the crest, and the lights of the tug boats floating on the river at its base. Down below, on my side of the river, was a flat floodplain on which an expanse of railroad tracks stretched along the river, lit up bright with white lights. A string of boxcars rolled slowly along the tracks, stopping with a shifting of boxcar couplings like dominoes down the line. Barges were lined up square and tight on the water. A heavy scaffolding of steel, from which a system of elevators and augers was suspended, transferred corn from the gravity boxes out onto the raft of barges with a low, constant grind of gears and motors. Guys could be seen moving over the barges, dragging tarps and directing the flow of corn, up to their knees and armed with shovels.

The sky had begun to clear. The clouds had thinned, and the stars were beginning to shine through the city lights. Cool air began to settle down into the valley, a breeze rolling down the bluffs and rustling the cottenwood

leaves. Frogs down in the marshy ravines chanted with a high pitched melody that repeated and rolled in over itself in waves that merged and diverged in constant, fluctuating streams of sound. An owl laughed eerily from the next ridge over, answered by another farther down the valley and I shivered, cold and with a sense of vulnerability. Not that I was afraid of the owls, but they can see in the dark and were probably watching me. Observing. I hate being observed more than anything. It makes me nervous. I was feeling insecure, anyways. Hungry. I missed supper. It was Tuesday, which meant meatloaf and mashed potatoes.

And the Mexican kid with the hairnet scoops extra gravy and I scowl as it runs into my peas, but he just smiles. He knows I like gravy. "A gravy loving menace," he says.

They'd be done eating by now, silverware rattling and the steamy hiss of the sprayers; trays clapping wet into stacks and the hollow sound of a ping-pong ball bouncing down the hallway linoleum.

Tuesdays are a big day around Heartsfield. Aside from being both laundry day and garbage day, we had meatloaf for dinner and afterwards there was a ping-pong tournament in the rec room. A lot of the patients spend hours practicing for the Tuesday night tournament, but it's all kind of pointless because of Hank.

Hank hasn't lost in over a year. He's big and soft but with reflexes derived from a dysfunctional nervous system. Someone drops a fork off their dinner tray and Hank is out of his chair from ten feet away and catches it before it hits the floor. Just sitting in the rec room watching tv and Hank leaps off the couch, snatching three, four flies out of the air in rapid succession, those big arms striking out like snakes. No one can beat him at ping-pong, unless there's flies in the room. Someone figured it out last summer and slashed the screens in the rec room, letting in so many flies Hank had a seizure during the Tuesday night tournament. Snatching flies and playing ping-pong and sweating and breathing harder till his eyes rolled and he fell over the table, breaking two of the legs. The staff suspended the tournaments until steel grates could be installed to protect the screens from further vandalism, and Hank hasn't lost since.

A steady, two beat rhythm drifted in beneath the chanting frogs, low and muffled. Tired, but unfaltering. Almost as if it were a heartbeat; a lone, tired heartbeat from deep in the shadows of the river bluffs. It came from the south, the direction of Ed's camp, near as I could tell in the swirling chanting of the frogs. Motivated by curiosity and misery, I picked up my suitcase and slid down into the next ravine. The air was cool and my clothes were soaked through and I couldn't stop shaking. The shakes can move anybody. If you don't think so, you've never had them. Not the ones I'm talking about.

Below the next ridge sat the sewer treatment plant, a brightly lit complex of culverts and long, narrow pools of water. The low hum of turbines vibrated like electricity and a faint odor of chlorine hung in the air. A chain link fence, 'No Trespassing' signs wired in the mesh, separated the mowed grass and sidewalks from the dark, tangled brush of the ravines. A path ran along the outside of the fence, worn through the brush, and I followed it south, careful to be quiet. Ed's camp lay close by, and appeared to be inhabited. The pounding was getting louder, and through the trees up ahead the glow of a fire could be seen. Cautiously, I approached thinking it might be a cult ritual of some kind.

Hardly breathing, I sneaked along the fence and came to the edge of a small clearing of tangled brush and grass. About forty feet away, the fire burned yellow, casting an uneven glow. It was Ed's camp, all right. Half a dozen sections of concrete sewer pipe lay scattered in the weeds like giant bones, about four feet high and ten feet long. Three of them were positioned with their black, gaping mouths converging like spokes on a wheel. At the hub burned the fire, around which lay three dogs: A big shaggy yellow one, which appeared to be sleeping; a little black one and a skinny white one, both of whom were busily gnawing on bones they held in their front paws. Nearby, a man was stomping aluminum cans.

He worked methodically, positioning two cans on the ground, smashing them with a quick thunk, thunk, one for each foot, then kicking them aside and reaching for two more off a pile in the weeds. His hair was long and grey, almost white, shining in the firelight. A tattered flannel shirt and baggy pants hung loose over his skinny frame. Despite the age suggested by his white hair, his movements were smooth and seemingly effortless, and he spoke to the dogs as he worked.

"One of you morons care to give me a hand?"

The dogs ignored him, except for the small black one, who raised her head and flapped her tail a few times, smiling at his joke. The big yellow one did not move, still stretched out on its side, while the skinny white one busied herself with the bone, pretending not to have heard him.

"Whoa, easy. Not all at once. Look, just forget I asked, ok? I'm almost done, anyways. No, really, I don't mind. Just relax, dammit."

Working steadily until the pile ran out, he kicked the last two cans aside and walked over to the fire, scratching the black dog's ears as he passed. From a pot of coffee resting near the fire, he poured himself a cup and settled down into a loose, busted up yellow lawn chair. Stretching out his legs, he stared into the flames.

It wasn't right to spy on him. Still, I hesitated to make my presence known. The man was dysfunctional. Perhaps unstable. There was no way of knowing how he might react to an intruder. We were outside the realm of law and order. Civilization offered no protection down here. But I was cold, and the warmth of the fire and the cozy campsite attracted my misery and it diffused through the air from an area of high concentration to one of low. That's how the dogs detected me. They smelled my misery.

The small black dog lept to its feet, head thrown back and howling like it'd been shot. The other two immediately followed, the yellow dog's bark loud and deep and the white one yapping high and fast, all three taking tenative steps in my direction.

With slow, measured movements, the old man lowered his cup of coffee and rolled cautiously from his chair into a low crouch on the ground, shifting his shoulders and craning his neck, trying to see into the shadows beyond the firelight.

"Who's out there?" he demanded, crouched behind a shield of snarling dogs.

My first impulse was to run, but there was no place to run to.

"A friend of Ed Ludgrin," I answered, regretting my response as soon as it was spoken. Ed wasn't much of a reference, if you really knew him.

"That don't tell me much," he said, and I felt better. "What do you want?" "Nothing," I lied, feeling a need to be cagey; not wanting to appear desperate.

"Ok. Now we're getting somewhere. Yes, that clarifies a lot."

His sarcastic tone struck a familiar note with the black dog, and she started grinning, wagging her tail and trotting out to greet me.

"Don't hurt Alice," he said, "She's a good dog. One of them dogs that figures everyone's her friend. Naive, I guess you could call her."

Alice moved quietly through the brush, appearing at my feet with a whine, tail beating and licking my hand in greeting. She damn near sat on my foot, leaning against my leg like we were old buddies. The old man waited on the ground, craning his neck at the shadows, trying to make me out, while the other two dogs barked mindlessly—loud and deep and high and fast. I wasn't sure what to do. Alice nudged my hand, so I scratched her ears a little, watching the man watching for me.

"What are you doing wandering around the bluffs in the middle of the night?"

Freezing my ass off. Good question. I'd been wondering that myself. I answered with a verbal shrug, instinctively volleying the question without committing myself.

"Nothing."

"You pick a strange time and place to do it."

"Actually, I'm looking for some shelter for the night," I admitted, starting to get the shakes again. Alice whined with concern, leaning warm and friendly against my leg.

"I imagine you would be. Miserable night to be sleeping in the bushes." Then he whistled sharp and immediately the two dogs quit barking, moving in close beside him. Alice got up to leave, but then thought the better of it and settled back down against my leg. I appreciated it, and reciprocated

with a good ear scratching.

Slowly, he got to his feet, refilling his cup of coffee. He sat back in his chair, stretching out his legs and lazily scratching an armpit.

"You got any money?" Silently, I cursed Ron. "Not much."

"Me too. I could use some, to be honest about it. And Alice seems to approve of you. She's not exactly what you'd call a smart dog. Neither are these other two, for that matter. Can't say I've ever really known a smart dog, in so far as a well rounded level of intelligence goes. But they're talented, each in their own way. You take Alice there. She's got a way with people—brings out the finer qualities of character, if in fact that person has some. The thing is, most people do have some fine qualities, just takes a special talent for rooting them out. Alice should be cloned, reproduced on a million petri dishes and scattered across the continent, and everyone could scratch her ears when they felt the need. Eliminate a lot of social ills, Alice would."

Alice sighed, luxuriating in the ear scratching I was giving her.

"She's a good dog", I agreed.

"That she is. Uncorrupted. Penniless and happy, unencumbered by frontal lobes. Don't know how to worry. How much money you got?"

"Not much," I repeated.

"Me too. Look, it's a miserable night to be sitting in the bushes. You can stay here. I'll set you up with a couple blankets, dry you out some. It's nothing fancy, but the coffee's hot and the whole night will only set you back a dollar. Better that sitting in the bushes."

It sounded like a reasonable offer and I would've accepted, except for the fact there was only eighty cents in my pocket.

"How much if I don't drink any coffee?"

The old guy rubbed his chin, pondering the situation. "It's a hard life, vagrancy. What can you afford?" "Seventy-five cents, no coffee."

He chuckled.

"Be worth seventy-five cents to get my Alice back. Coffee's free. C'mon in."

"Shut the hell up, Clyde."

The big yellow dog sat across the fire from me, every minute or so barking loud, directly into my face. The old guy was getting a kick out of it, as were the dogs. Everyone was grinning. Clyde would wait until he thought I'd let my guard down, then startle me with a loud, deep blast, delighting in the response he got got from my raw nerves. Alice and Sadie, the white dog, were as close to giggling as a dog can get, swooning over big Clyde's audacity.

"You like cream?" the guy asked, pouring me a steaming cup. "Just a touch," I replied.

"Me too." He said, handing me the cup, black.

Alice and Sadie grinned over at me with amusement while he tossed a couple chunks of wood on the fire.

"Gotta warm you up. Them clothes you're wearing are out of context.

You got anything drier in that bag of yours?"

There were a couple pair of greens in my suitcase, but they would've prompted too many questions. Besides, they were just thin, cotton pajamas. "Don't matter to me", he said, scratching an armpit. "Just stand close and dry yourself out. You're young, but that don't mean you can't get sick. How'd you end up down here, anyways?"

The man appeared to be afflicted by some sort of nervous disorder, his hands betraying an inner anxiety despite his relaxed outward appearance. They twitched and roamed his body, pinching at his clothing and scratching continuously.

"I knew a guy who used to live down here. He told me about these sewer tunnels and how he used to catch fish and cook them on a fire. I just came down here to see, looking to get out of the rain. He said no one ever came down here."

"He was right on that point. Did you say his name was Ed?" "Yeah. Ed Ludgrin. You know him?"

He poked at the fire. The flames were growing stronger, casting a brighter glow about the clearing. Little curls of steam rose from my wet clothes as the warmth began to soak through. I moved in as close as I could, almost giddy with relief.

"Never met him. These tunnels were empty when I found them. Three years this spring. Guy half a mile up the river talks about him now and then, though. Used to fish together. Charles says this Ed Ludgrin was a poet."

"He won a Pulitzer." I said, almost proud of the little runt, but the old man showed no appreciation, scratching his scalp and checking his fingernails.

"He wrote some things in the tunnels. Must've laid in there on rainy days with a piece of chalk. Mostly smeared out now. A lot of nonsense, most of it. There's one line I liked, though. Committed it to memory. He wrote 'The Universe is simply a matter of moments.' Kind of a nice veiw, I thought."

It sounded like Ed. Ed thought of moments like a chemist thinks of molecules.

"He was crazy," I felt compelled to declare. I can't say I'm jealous of Ed, but it was irritating to hear him quoted all the time, as though he were something special.

"Don't doubt that. Gotta be, living in a sewer tunnel."

The fire cracked and snapped, throwing off embers that glowed for a moment before cooling into the mud at my feet. The warm glow of the fire spread out across the clearing. Around the gaping black mouths of the nearby tunnels the ground was worn bare from regular use. Further out, tangles of thorny berry canes grew wild, trailing over and almost burrying some sections of tunnel. Beyond the firelight the tree covered bluffs rose steep and dark, the lights of the city shining over the crest.

"Charles said this Ed was committed to an insane asylum." He spoke in an innocent tone, as though not insinuating anything. A warm wave washed over me, and it wasn't just the fire.

"Easy, son. Don't matter to me. You're here now, and you gotta dry out. We'll get you fixed up for the night. Sky's cleared off, and tomorrow the sun will be shining. You'll feel better with some sunshine on your day. Looks like you could use some. My name's Franklin, by the way."

He poked at the fire, and the moment hung awkward.

'Why do you continue to stay, that is my question?' Six years. Voluntary.

Menace, what a joke.

Franklin shrugged off the moment. "Don't matter."

"Ed Ludgrin is dead." Franklin poked at the fire.

"Sorry to hear. Can't say I'm surprised, though. He had his nose stuck in it. Probably got run over by a truck."

I tried not to smile, but failed. "You good at sleeping?"

I just shrugged, having never thought about it before.

"I been holed up all day, on account of the weather. Slept most of it. Warm and dry and listening to the rain. I'd sleep through the night, if I could. When I was your age, I could. Just lay there and dream. That's the trouble with getting old. You get pratical. Used to be I'd damn near starve for a dream. No more. I'm hungry."

Suddenly the white dog had a seizure, jumping up and sitting down, dragging herself around the fire, sort of walking on her front legs, stiff and strained. It was frightening. She headed for me and I backed away, thinking it might be rabies.

"She's got worms. Nothing to be afraid of. Just miserable for poor Sadie. Cost me three-fifty for the pills, and I ain't got it. Not yet, anyways. It's a hard life, vagrancy. Not complaining, just that I've got obligations. She's a good dog, and I'll get it. Another week and I'll have enough."

Sadie calmed down and lay once more by the fire, chewing on a bare bone. She was skin and bones, and it dawned on me Franklin was talking about intestinal parasites. He watched her chewing hard on damn near nothing.

"Look, the dogs are hungry and so am I. We're going to swing up Brewery Street. There'll be activity tonight. Always is after an all day rain. Let's get you set up before we leave."

He crawled into one of the near by tunnels, rummaging around in the dark, and came backing out dragging a pile of dirty blankets.

'You can have 3B," he said, indicating a tunnel off in the weeds, as though there were guys sleeping in the other ones. "And don't worry. It's dark as hell in there, but the dogs keep the skunk and 'coon out, and it's too early for bees."

I began to worry.

"Now, the fire will be strong for another half hour, so dry yourself out good before crawling in. It'll be easier to fall asleep if you dry out, and you're gonna need every advantage you can get. Tunnels weren't designed for comfort. Lay a couple blankets under you and cover up with the rest."

He retrieved an old gunny sack from beside the pile of flattened cans and the three dogs gathered around, whining and wagging their tails, looking excited.

"We'll be back by morning. Finish off the coffee if you want, and set the pot off to the side so it don't scorch. Ok, you morons, let's go."

And the dogs bounced along the chain link fence, yelping and chasing through the brush, followed by Franklin and his dirty old sack.

"Shut up, Clyde."

And Clyde's response broke loud and deep, mixing in with the sound of a diesel coming down the east bank approach, downshifting and airbraking for the Brewery Street Bridge, a quarter of a mile up the river, the sound rolling down through the valley like thunder.

Dark and heavy the thunder passed, and in its wake rose the sounds of the riverbluff night. The low grind of the augers mixed with the hum of the turbines, forming a grey base. A constant, grey buzz over which the frogs chirped in bright shades of red. Thousands of frogs, the sheer volume over- whelming my senses, growing in intensity. Thousands and thousands of them, surrounding me and in constant communication. I felt very much alone and kept a nervous eye on the outer perimeter of the firelight, half expecting to see a trickle of dark frogs creeping down from the shadows, followed by hordes of deranged frogs hopping out of the brush, attracted to the light of the fire, wet and slimy and crawling over each other, swarming down on the camp and smothering everything in their path.

At least there weren't any skunks or raccoons or bees in the sewer tunnel.

At least there weren't, last time anyone looked.

Eventually, I began to worry about the fire. The flames died down into a red glow of embers and the circle of firelight began to shrink. The fire meant a lot to me. The night began to close in, bringing with it isolation and uncertainty. Franklin had a stick beside his chair for poking the fire, and I tried to ignite one end and use it as a torch to search for more wood, figuring he must have a cache nearby. The torch idea didn't work, though, because everytime I turned from the fire, the torch died and the stick just glowed red, offering no light and I stumbled around in the weeds and brush, getting soaked. I happened to stumble over one stick about the size of my leg, but it was so wet it did more harm than good to the fading campfire. My pants were soaked clear through. Disgusted, I gathered my blankets and headed out for 3B.

"Hey!" I yelled into the pitch black hole, my voice sounding distant and hollow. There was no telling what was in there, waiting silently. I tried to listen for the sound of breathing, but the frogs were louder than ever and if anything was in there, waiting, it'd probably be holding its breath anyways. Retrieving a rock from the fire ring, I yelled again and threw it inside, jumping back in case something came charging out. Nothing happened, though, and Franklin was probably right—there probably wasn't anything to worry about. Still, I backed in feet first, shoving the suitcase ahead of me to blunt any attack.

Following Franklin's instructions, I laid two blankets on the floor of the tunnel and covered up with the others. The smell of dog was thick, and if you've ever slept in a culvert, you know it was not easy for me to fall asleep. The tunnel was wide enough to lay in, but hard as a rock and it was difficult to roll over. I had to sort of spin myself in place and the coffee was making me toss and turn, forcing me to crawl out and take a leak a couple of times and although exhausted, I could not fall asleep. I kept listening for the night nurse to pass by the door, her rubber soled shoes squeaking on the linoleum. Instead, the sound of the sewer turbines and the frogs and augers grinding filled the air. Traffic rumbled across the valley, diesel trucks downshifting for the Brewery Street Bridge, and a siren howled distant and lonely.

My routine had been disrupted. I'd spent enough time in the institution to appreciate the value of having a routine. The first thing the staff did for a new resident was outline the day's agenda, establishing a routine for breakfast, group meetings, ping-pong tournaments. They even posted the entire week's menue every Monday morning, so residents would know what they were having for desert at Thursday night's supper. It was a secure environment.

In a way, the sewer tunnel was secure. I was out of sight. That alone was my only comfort.

The fact that I was lying in a sewer tunnel bothered me. More than it should have. It was secure, but it was a secure sewer tunnel, none-the-less. The fact that nobody could see me did not alter the truth.

The world is viewed differently from inside of a sewer tunnel. It is out there, over there, beyond the mouth of the tunnel. One is separated from the world and able to view it from a detached viewpoint. In a way, it might be like dying. A sewer tunnel provides solitude and time for reflection. Perhaps not peaceful reflection. I was berating myself for being an idiot. Cursing myself, questioning, wondering how I could have been such a moron. I tore myself apart, reduced to the point of tears. But reflection is good for the soul. Tears are a catharsis. You cannot judge a man based on the fact that at a certain point in his life he had to seek shelter in a sewer tunnel. Perhaps it's not for everyone, but spending some time in quiet reflection of the truth can be enlightening.

It can be Miserable at the time, though. If you've been there, you understand. If you haven't, you won't. I'm not going to argue about it.

The low, foggy sound of a tugboat woke me up. Or at least began the awakening process. What really brought me around were the fleas. Hundreds of them, burrowing beneath my clothes. It was disgusting. Not to mention uncomfortable. Fleas bite like hell, and the bites itch. My body was alive with them, a virtual colony of fleas. My body was the food source for a colony of fleas. It was a disgusting thought. The air of the tunnel was thick with dog. Directly above me, on the ceiling of the concrete tunnel, a chalk scrawled message from Ed greeted me.

Cherish the moment.

My body ached from the absolute hardness of the concrete. Flat on my back, unable to even roll over, with several hundred fleas calling my body home, I began to hunch and push, inchworming towards the weeds at the mouth of the tunnel. Drops of water sprinkled down into my face as I hunched out, gasping for cool, fresh air as though breaking surface after a long, deep dive in muddy water.

The sun was just breaking over the eastern bluffs, reaching across the valley and sliding down the steep hill behind me. I was tempted to climb up and meet it, but the sun rose quickly and the warm rays were soon reaching into the depths of the valley. Traffic was heavy on the Brewery Street Bridge, and the augers were grinding down at the loading docks. The hum of the turbines was constant, and more obvious without the bright red chirping of the frogs. The Silent Frogs.

The smell of woodsmoke surprised me. The fire had smoldered all night, eating into the log I'd found in the weeds. Burnt in half, the ends of the log lay on either side of a pile of white ashes and underneath, the ashes were still hot. Flopping the two chunks of wood on the embers, I got down on my knees and began to blow and in a few minutes the smoke thinned out into a brand new flame.

I lit a cigarette and felt the smug satisfaction of a survivor for the first time. It was a cocky feeling, a light footed spiritness that made me want to move. Stutter stepping, feinting, jabbing at the air around me, knocking the world on its ass. Grabbing Franklin's poker stick, I became the lead guitar player for the killer new band, The Silent Frogs. Grimacing, I rock and rolled around the fire, making my guitar scream. The bluff was transformed into a giant stadium filled with thousands of young women out of their minds with desire. Then a flea bit me behind the ear, shattering my illusion of grandeur.

I was smoking and pacing in circles, chasing down fleas and ruthlessly dropping them into the fire, when the sound of aluminum cans came rattling down along the chain link fence. The three dogs broke from the brush, were momentarily taken aback by my presence, then erupted into a spasm of loud barking, circling around, trying to catch my scent. Franklin was coming down the path, sack slung over his shoulder and giving the dogs hell.

"You bone headed morons, you've got the memory of a rock. Yes, we have a guest, so shut already. It's common knowledge, dammit, shut up."

Clyde registered a few more objections, but then shut up and sat down next to Sadie, both scratching themselves with a hind foot. Alice came forward with a happy smile, sniffed my foot and wagged her tail up at me.

"Good morning, son. I trust you slept safely, if not well."

Franklin didn't look particularly dysfunctional in the light of day, despite his loose, shapeless clothing. His white hair implied wisdom, and he seemed relaxed and confident. Content. Yet contentment is a rare trait, often associated with mild retardation, the exception being primitive cultures, in which contentment is far more common. Contentment in America was rare by the end of the twentieth century. Not surprisingly, I resented it and started giving him hell about the fleas, but he just waved off my complaints.

"Hell, fleas won't kill you. Pretty soon you build up a tolerance and hardly notice them," he said, scratching his scalp. "Besides, what do you expect for seventy-five cents? You got a place to sleep, and breakfast to boot."

With that, he opened up his sack and pulled out the ugliest animal I'd ever seen. It looked like a rat. A big, white faced rat. Its teeth were bared in a sharp, cynical smile—dried blood around its ugly nose. The dogs gathered around enthusiastically, wagging their tails and reaching up with their noses to examine the beast. Franklin held forth the animal. I believe he expected me to handle it in admiration.

"What is it?" I asked.

"Possum!" he exclaimed. "First possum I ever record. They're not common this far north, you know. Could indicate a shifting in climatic regions, could be a hardy strain of possum. Could be a fluke. Dogs found it up on Third Street, in the alley behind Stacey's. Possums are slow. Probably a beer truck got it. Not bad, though, and it was still warm."

The term 'still warm' made me uneasy. He could just as well have said 'still soft.' I asked him what he was going to do with it.

"Stew!" Franklin answered. "Stew the meat and register the skull."

He dropped the possum to the ground and went off rummaging in one of the tunnels while the dogs stood protectively over the animal. They seemed torn between grabbing it and running or keeping the other two from doing so. Franklin returned with a wood crate about the size of my suitcase, a hatchet and a knife. With the movements of an experienced butcher, he prepared the possum for stew.

Although my initial reaction was revulsion, the deftness of his thick fingers became fascinating. With almost childlike enthusiasm, he handled his rare specimen as though it were a wrapped gift. Setting two kettles of water on the fire grate, he dropped the carcass into the larger, along with a sprinkling of green herbs and a potato. The head of the possum went into the other. It made me light headed. I sat down on the crate, watching the water beginning to boil. Franklin soon rousted me, though. The crate contained part of his skull collection, which he was anxious to show me.

It was shocking, at first, all those empty eye sockets and bare teeth. Stacks of bleached white skulls, each with a little number painted on top. There were squirrel skulls and rabbit skulls and muskrat and mice and chipmonk and even a goat skull. Franklin was soon absorbed in a narrative on skulls of particular interest, such as the goat, which he figured had fallen from a stock- yard truck. He passed some of the skulls to me. They were clean and dry and I guess interesting, but I had to ask.

"Why, Franklin?"

He evaded my question. Or misunderstood. "They're my data base."

Franklin was conducting a scientific survey of Nocturnal Urban Rodents. And marsupials, if it really matters. The numbers on the skulls corresponded to an index file he kept in a thick, loose leaf binder. He recorded several measurements of pertinent interest to his survey, along with the date and location of each specimen. There were several more crates hidden away in the tunnels, and Franklin knew the contents of each.

Franklin returned the skulls to the crate and turned his attention to making coffee. He dumped a scoop of grounds into the steaming pot, and the smell rose fresh and moist.

I was confused. About much more than Franklin's skull collection, but he had my immediate attention. I asked again.

"But why, Franklin?"

He was hunched over the coffee pot, inhaling fumes. He answered with a shrug of his shoulders.

"In my blood, I guess."

Suffering an identity crisis of my own, I felt compelled to identify Franklin's personality make-up. It's a lot easier to categorize someone else than it is yourself. It's hard to be objective when you're dealing with emotions. Humiliation is an emotion. It certainly feels like one, anyways. Casually, I sat back down on the crate, gently prodding for more information.

"What's in your blood, Franklin?"

He was poking at the fire with his stick, arranging the coals into little piles beneath the kettles of boiling possum. With a sigh, he rolled back on his heels, absently scratching his head and looking out across the valley.

"The gathering of knowledge," he said in a tired voice. "Franklins have been interested in the gathering of knowledge for generations. Perhaps you've heard of my namesake, the most famous kite flyer in the history of our great nation? The man whose discovery of electricity altered the course of evolution on this planet more swiftly and profoundly than any discovery in the previous 50,000 years of human existence? I'm a Franklin, son, and I feel the responsibility of knowledge. The gathering of it, primarily, along with its wise use."

Franklin poured us each another cup of coffee. Either he actually believed he was Ben Franklin's great something or other grandson, or he was playing me for a fool. Either way, he was crazy—for believing it, or for thinking I would. Playing along cool as pudding, I asked him what benefit he felt his knowledge held for mankind.

Franklin was a very forward looking man. Crazy

as hell, though. He saw himself as operating on a very small spot on a very large rung of the prehistoric and possibly, at least, infinite evolutionary ladder. If each generation made notes about the world around them and passed them on to the next, knowledge, and he reasoned, wisdom, would grow expotentially until perhaps someday humanity could learn the ultimate lesson: How to live in a peaceful world governed by morals derived from generational wisdom. Like I said, Franklin was a very forward looking man. By the end of his explanation, I knew he was a crazy bastard. Poor crazy bastard. No one gives a damn about nocturnal urban rodents, unless they're causing property damage.

He was pretty smart, though, for a crazy bastard. I was starting to feel better. The sun was warm, and in the sunshine a flock of yellow butterflies fluttered over a small puddle of rainwater, praying on its shores with folded wings. A dragonfly, metallic blue with bulging eyes and long legs, landed on my knee, its body poised and stiff, its wings tensed. I'd never seen one before and it looked like it was going to sting me. I jumped up, swatting at it, spilling coffee on my crotch and scattering butterflies. Franklin was laughing.

"Hell, dragonfly isn't going to hurt you. Just stopping by to say hello."

There were dozens of dragonflies darting around the weeds. Green and blue. Some were big, others were just little things. They darted like sprinters over the weeds. I was just standing around, watching the dragonflies, when I got this strange sensation and looking out across the clearing, I saw somebody. Partially hidden in the willows on the edge of the clearing, a guy was watching us. He was big, wearing shaded glasses and a dark suit; just standing there, looking at us.

"Franklin," I said, "There's a guy in the brush over there, watching us." Franklin's head came up quick and the dogs lifted their heads and whined,

unsure of what was wrong.

"Who is it?" Franklin spoke in a half-wisper. The dogs got to their feet, whining, unable to scent the guy out in the willows.

"I think it's a bodyguard."

Franklin moaned. "Damn, I should've known. Son, who's your daddy? You're breaking his heart. Go on back, boy, he's worried about you. And take your damn babysitter with you."

The dogs picked scent and erupted into a violent fit of barking. Another guy stepped out of the brush on the far side of the clearing; just standing there, looking at us. Big guy, with a dark suit and shaded glasses.

Suddenly there was the sound of laughter from up the chain link path. Out of the willows stepped a guy with a tv camera, walking backwards. Several other people with small cases strapped over their shoulders followed. Some were holding microphones and some were holding cameras and in the middle of the crowd, smiling broad and friendly, was Mayor Mckinnley himself. He was waving at Franklin and me like he knows us and is glad to have finally found us.

"That your daddy, son? My Lord, what is he? Some sort of movie star?" I was as confused as Franklin.

"That's the mayor." I said. Franklin misunderstood.

"I'll be damned," he said, shaking his head and placing his hand on my shoulder. "Not much of a resemblance."

The mayor was getting closer. The dogs' barking was reaching a feverish pitch.

"Franklin, the man doesn't know me from Noah. I have no idea what he wants."

Franklin looked at me, saw I wasn't lying, and his eyes widened.

"I'll be damned." Then he started digging into his crate and pulled out the goat skull, holding it up in front of him. The mayor was just coming across the bare ground around the fire ring, and at the sight of the goat skull, he pulled up short, a look of confusion and mild alarm on his face.

It could be that within each of us lies a yearning to be understood, and in a small, perhaps selfish way, appreciated. Franklin must've thought the mayor had heard about his skull collection and wanted to see it. So with a stupid grin, he held the goat skull forward, offering it as some kind of gift, apparently.

The mayor recognized the symbolism of the gift offering, and his face brightened into a smile. With the cameras flashing and the dogs sniffing at his shoes, he stepped forward with dignity usually reserved for heads of state, humbly accepting the goat skull with a bow of his head. Beaming, he turned to face the cameras, holding up the skull.

"We've got a bone to pick with the Republicans, ladies and gentlemen." Although unsettling, the mayor's hair no longer appeared dangerous.

It seemed to be clinging fearfully to his head, afraid of slipping and falling into the clutches of the three dogs barking up at it. Red dots flickered on the tv cameras with a sense of urgency. Franklin was scratching his head in bewilderment, and all I could do was stand there with my hands folded passively over my crotch, the reporters looking at us like we're both crazy, a hint of disgust on their faces. The mayor was presenting a speech.

"Why is it that the Republicans don't want dental care for everyone in our society, from the most prestigious banker down to the most miserable misfits surviving on the fringes of society, stuck in a rut of misery and squalor? Greed is the answer. For who but the greedy accumulate wealth of obscene proportions? Here we have a man, destitute, yet offering me his most prized possession."

He held up the goatskull again, eliciting a nervous giggle from the reporters. Franklin was perplexed when the mayor asked him how long it'd been since he'd seen a dentist, just kind of shrugging his shoulders. So the mayor asked me and I lied and said eight years, even though they checked our teeth every three months at Heartsfield.

"Eight years! Did you hear that? Eight years since Mr Jones has been to a dentist. It's obscene, friends. Remember—there but for the grace of God Himself, or Herself, for that matter, go I. For whatever you do to the least of my brothers, or sisters, that you do unto me."

Then he launched into his festering wound speech, the one I'd heard the day before by the brewery. He seemed to be empowered by the goat skull, waving it emphatically to stress certain points, his voice rising and falling dramatically. It had a mesmerizing effect. A very powerful moment. Unfortunately for the mayor, and much more so for Sadie, she had an attack of worms. Whining, she sat down and began dragging herself across the trampled grass, a strained look on her face.

It was distracting as hell. The reporters giggled nervously. The mayor looked around to see what the problem was.

"She's got worms," Franklin said, by way of explanation. Everyone just kind of stood there, watching the dog. The mayor, sensing his loss of momentum, tried to regain control. Clearing his throat, he pointed the goat skull at the suffering dog.

"Even the dogs are miserable. Even the dogs suffer miserably, living in such squalor. Do we allow our brothers, the poor miserable misfits of society, to live like dogs?"

I was starting to resent the hell out of the mayor, but felt vulnerable with my wet crotch. Nothing is more discrediting than a wet crotch.

"Hey," Franklin yelled at the poor dog, "We've got company. Where's your manners?" He stomped his foot threateningly. "Knock it off."

Poor Sadie wimpered and trotted off into the weeds to suffer in private. The Mayor resumed his speech, but no one was paying attention. We were all watching the bodyguard out in the weeds. He was afraid of the dragonflies buzzing around him. He was swatting at them, ducking and dodging whenever one flew in too close.

"Hell, dragonflies won't hurt you," Franklin yelled. The bodyguard realized everyone was watching and stoically stood his ground, but flinching when approached by the mean looking bugs. By now the mayor had lost all momentum and was smart enough to realize it. He handed the goat skull back to Franklin.

"Let us move on, ladies and gentlemen. Let us carry our message back up into the streets. And higher still, into the corporate offices at the top of societies ladder. For while we gain insight down here in the mud, it makes for unsure footing. One loses sight of the distant horizons, and despair rots the soul. Let us go fight for those less fortunate than ourselves. And so we leave you, Mr Franklin and Mr Jones, not to die in your misery, but to survive, until the day comes when we can return and offer you a helping hand, to lift you to a higher standard of living. Thank you."

He shook our hands again, red dots flickering on the cameras and the dogs barking, ignoring Franklin's threats. The mayor led his crowd back down the chain link fence path, several of the reporters glancing back at Franklin and myself, a couple of misfits. The bodyguards were gone. They melted back into the willows as quietly as they had appeared. Franklin poured himself a cup of coffee and offered me some.

"Now what the hell do you suppose that was all about?" he asked, staring down the empty path. I was disgusted.

"I thought you said no-one ever came down here." Franklin just shrugged.

"That's usually the case. Can't say I understand it myself. Must be some kind of crusade. They're hard to predict. Probably nothing to worry about. Crusades usually run their courses pretty quick."

Franklin moved about the fire adding wood, adjusting the steaming pots.

I sat smoking and brooding, trying to decide on a course of action. I felt some basic right of mine had been violated.

"I'd be surprised if the mayor was to turn up again anytime soon. 'Course, I'm surprised he turned up at all. That's the thing about crusades-unpredictable as hell. Nice day, though. Actually, it's a fine day for a crusade. Spring green fresh sunshine, and a simmering stew. Just look at the river. Makes a man feel good, don't it? Hell yes, it's a fine day for a crusade, if I'm any judge."

He was right. About the river, I mean. It was beautiful, with the morning sunshine on it. It sparkled. A fresh breeze was blowing and the water rippled. A raft of barges was headed downriver, the crew checking lines and leaning against the rails. Peaceful as hell. Still, I couldn't shake my feeling of resentment toward the mayor for using us like that.

"If he wants me to join his crusade, the least he could do is ask first, rather than charging in here like some kind of damn savior."

Franklin just shrugged.

"It'd take too long to ask everyone first. No one gives a damn what you think about it, anyways. It's the mayor's crusade."

"You can't own a damn crusade." Franklin shrugged again.

"I don't know about crusades. They're unpredictable. Besides, that ain't the point."

"Well, just what the hell is the point?" I demanded an explanation for the grotesque example of exploitation I'd just witnessed.

Franklin sighed, threw a few more sticks on the fire, then got up and crawled into one of the tunnels, emerging with a filthy brown blanket. Shaking it in the breeze, scattering clouds of dog hair and dust, he laid the blanket on the ground and sat on it. Then he looked at me in an amused, sympathetic way. "The point is, son, is that it's a fine day." Leaning back, he stretched out for a nap in the warm sunshine, folding his hands over his chest, within minutes snoring softly. One by one the dogs started yawning and stretching and wandering off into the weeds, turning circles before settling down. Soon I was surrounded by the snoring of three old dogs and one old man, all flea bitten, social misfits. Pathetic.

Nobody said anything as I dragged my suitcase out of the tunnel and stood waiting for someone to. Alice lifted her head in the weeds, her tail flapping, but that was it. I knew Franklin was awake, because he was no longer snoring. Probably had been faking it the whole time. But he didn't make a move to say goodbye, and so I left without a word, resenting him and the damn Mayor and my stupid suitcase and even

Alice, wagging her tail like an idiot. I resented the damn sunshine, and the fact that it was such a nice day and I wasn't in the mood to enjoy it. Heading back up the path, along the chain link fence, I retraced my steps from the night before, making a mental list of everything I resented and cursing the hell out of each as I thought of them. It was actually pretty amazing. Everyone I knew or had ever met was either an idiot or a son of a bitch. Misled, misjudged, betrayed—a victim of ignorance and incompetence.

Eventually I found myself back up in the ravines, where the big cotton- woods grow. The leaves of the top-most branches flickered and whispered. A soothing sound, like a waterfall. Wrinkled rough and deep, the big trees looked wise, and I related to them. I even hugged one, just to see how far my arms reached around. It would've taken at least three guys to do it.

Nearing the Brewery Street Bridge, I followed a ridge up through the bluffs, intent on relocating the brewery before making any decisions. I wasn't sure where to go from there, but I needed a place to start. I needed to know where I stood.

At the top of the bank was the little park with a couple of benches and trash cans stuffed with styrofoam cups. Just a little corner of green grass mowed short, a few oak trees, and an historical plaque mounted in granite, commemorating a battle that took place between the Ojibaway and Chippewa Indian Nations two hundred years ago. It'd been a territorial dispute. Many men had died and if you look close around on the ground, you might get lucky and find an arrowhead. Of course, the park isn't very big and the bulk of the battle zone now lay under the brewery parking lot.

The reason I stood there and read the sign so close was because there were about twenty guys standing around in the park, yellow hardhats on their heads and lunch boxes in hand, drinking coffee out of little styrofoam cups and eating sweetrolls. They were kind of looking at me, the guy in the sportsuit with the big suitcase who'd just climbed out of the woods.

I felt self-conscious and just stood looking at the plaque awhile, trying to decide what to do. The guys were standing around in little groups, talking and glancing over at me, laughing at a joke between them. An old Buick station wagon was parked off to one side and a woman was standing by the tailgate, polishing a chrome coffee maker and shooing flies off a couple of boxes of sweetrolls. She wore a grey carpenter's apron and bluejeans, her brown hair held back with a red bandanna. She looked bored as hell, pouring out refills and polishing her coffee maker.

It appeared to be an informal gathering, and since I hadn't eaten in twenty-four hours, I decided to find out how much she wanted for a bismark. She ignored me, standing there with my suitcase. Most of the guys did too, except for some snickering. I couldn't blame them. I knew I looked ridiculous. Still, I resented it. It's a free country, and I didn't look any dumber than them, with their yellow hardhats. But I was outnumbered, and just stood quietly by the tailgate looking at the boxes of rolls till finally she had to say something, though hardly bothering to look at me.

"Fresh box is on the right, forty-five cents apiece. Day-old on the left, twenty cents. No giveaways."

I was really starting to resent her attitude. I wasn't looking for a damn handout. Still, I couldn't act too cocky with only eighty cents in my pocket. Silently I cursed Ron, and asked for a custard long-john out of the day-old box. "They aren't custard," she said, as though irritated by the request, "custard always go on the first day. The ones left over don't have any filling."

She kept on polishing her coffee maker like she was wishing I'd just go away. I felt a flea in my armpit and started to chase it. She got this disgusted look on her face, and I pretended to be just brushing some lint off my suit.

"I'll take a plain long-john out of the day-old box," I said, as though it really didn't matter, and it was childish of her to even make an issue out of it. She sighed and handed me the stale roll on a napkin. I dug out twenty cents and she dropped the change into her apron and just as I was about to wolf it down, I remembered the seventy-five cents I hadn't paid Franklin for sleeping in the culvert. It was a hell of a dilemma. I thought about Sadie and how miserable with worms she was. I had an obligation to pay. Franklin would think me a bum. I had to go back and pay him, for the sake of both the white dog and my principles.

I felt stupid having to ask for my money back. But there was only sixty cents left and besides, I hadn't yet taken a bite.

"What?" she said, pausing in her polishing, as though she couldn't have heard right.

"I can't afford it. I'd like to give it back for a refund." She kinda snorted through her nose at me.

"What are you trying to pull, anyways? I don't want the damn thing.

You bought it, it's yours."

I felt trapped. "Look," I said, "I owe someone seventy-five cents and they're counting on it and if I buy this, I won't be able to even up."

She looked at me with a cynically bored expression on her face, then lit a cigarette and blew smoke, squinting her eyes and looking mean. Her name was Rose and she never smoked unless she was mad about something. I didn't know that yet.

The rest of the guys did. They'd been keeping an eye on us anyways, and when they saw Rose light a cigarette, they started milling in closer to see what the matter was. I was getting nervous. This big guy, with a big red face, came pushing through the crowd, spilling coffee with his big belly sticking out tight in his t-shirt.

"What's the problem, Rose?" he asked in this big, loud voice that quieted everyone down.

Rose raised her chin at me. "Bum wants his money back."

It was embarrassing as hell. The big guy looks at me, my dirty sports suit and the big suitcase. He looks at me a moment, like he might know me or something, and everyone's quiet to see what he's going to do. I was wishing I could get out of there, but the guys are gathered in close now around the tailgate, and the big guy is right in front of me.

But he don't say anything. He's just looking at me, then he looks at Rose, and his face starts to lighten up. He looks back at me and cleared his throat like he was going to say something important, but instead he starts giggling and spilling coffee on his big belly, he's getting such a kick out of it.

Everyone kinda chuckles then and started backing away into their little groups, forgetting about me and Rose pours out a few refills and sells some rolls out of the fresh box, shoos off some flies and goes back to polishing her coffee maker like she don't give a damn about any of it. The big guy's name was Murphy and he was still giggling, standing there with the styrofoam cup looking ridiculously small in his big hand.

"Sorry, buddy," he says, putting a hand on my shoulder, "But around here, Rose is right, and that's the bottom line."

I resented the hell out of him laughing at me. I tried to leave, to go back down and settle up with Franklin as well as I could, but Murphy still had a hand on my shoulder and stopped me.

He quit laughing and looked me in the eye. "I'll buy that damn roll from ya, buddy."

I was mad and got this real bored look on my face, like none of it mattered to me at all.

"It's not for sale," I said, jerking my shoulder free and pushing past him. Halfway down the riverbank, I could still hear his laughter booming loud and deep.

It was a relief to be back under the spell of the rustling cottonwoods, Murphy's laughter finally fading away. Dragging my suitcase up a ridge, I found a sunny rock and sat down to eat. The roll was stale and dry as hell. Down on the floodplain, an engine pulled a long line of boxcars, creeping up to the loading docks. There was a raft of barges lined up straight and square on the water, and the augers were grinding low. Guys were walking around the docks and driving forklifts, and I would've given anything to have a job like that—with probably a wife and a couple kids and the kids have a cat they carried around the backyard like a baby. Instead, I'd just spent the night in a sewer tunnel, crawling with fleas with nowhere to go.

And dying from embarrassment, sitting there watching the trains creeping along the tracks. I'd sauntered around Heartsfield like a menace for six years, making a complete ass of myself. Hormonal imbalance, for Christ's sake. Just what in the hell were the Staff's instructions for dealing with the kid in 14A? Watch out for that Emerson, he's got hair popping out all over the place. I hated Eric Whitebird and Judge Marshal. A couple of bozos, playing God, I swear. I felt terrible. The fleas were chewing the hell out of me. I thought about dying. Right there, sitting on that rock, watching the trains down below and the pigeons swooping down off the Brewery Street Bridge. Then I thought of Franklin and his dogs, and knew it'd be a mistake to die down there. I'd end up next to the goat skull, with a little number painted on my head.

And the next time the mayor stopped in, Franklin would haul me out and present me as a token of his insanity. And because of Heartsfield's dental records, everyone would know it was me. Franklin standing there with a proud smile, holding my skull on the evening news.

So I just sat smoking and watching the pigeons, determined not to enjoy the day. I'd had it with people. Just a bunch of crazy bastards, I swear.

There must have been five hundred pigeons swarming around the docks. Most of them were grey, but every now and then a brown and white one flashed in the sun. They looked clean, the brown and white ones. They looked brand new.

Apparently a large number of pigeons were nesting up in the steel webbing and bracing on the Brewery Street Bridge. It was a huge bridge, stretching half a mile across the valley, over the railroad tracks and the river. Every now and then a big diesel truck rumbled across the bridge, downshifting and groaning, trying to lose momentum as the traffic slowed for the intersection on first street. As the trucks roared overhead, pigeons swooped down from the bridgework, as though shaken loose from their nests.

It was relaxing, watching the pigeons and listening to the cottonwoods, and I was starting to feel better, when all of a sudden I see somebody dangling from the bridge—out over the railroad tracks, fifty feet in the air, hanging by his hands from a steel girder beam, kicking his legs wildly while pigeons swarmed around in a cloud of excitement. Fifty feet in the air, with nothing but steel and solid ground below.

I just stood there a moment, unsure what I was witnessing. 911 flashed in my head. 911, 911. But there wasn't any telephone. So at the top of my lungs, just to relieve tension, I yelled '911,' then grabbed my suitcase and started running down the path. I had no idea what

I could do to help, but I couldn't just sit there and watch him fall.

It was stupid, but as I was running, I kept thinking about how great it would be if I could save the guy. How good it would look, I mean, to the people back at Heartsfield, and especially Angela. I know it's stupid, but I kept envisioning myself in tomorrow's paper, looking cool and bored, shaking hands with the guy I'd saved like it was nothing at all for me to do something heroic.

It was only a couple hundred yards but the path was uneven, up and down into the ravines. At one point there was a marshy swamp-hole, filled with green water and weeds, and the only way across was a dead tree lying over it. The trunk was shiny smooth from all the feet that had shuffled across.

In the middle of the span sat half a dozen turtles, catching some of the early rays. I yelled '911' and dashed across. They panicked and disappeared into the green water with hardly a splash. It was exhilarating to be on a mission like that. Step aside for lunatics and heroes. Heroes have the right-of-way. Lunatics think they do.

"911" I yelled again, breaking from the brush out onto the grassy clearing near the foot of the bridge.

"Thank God you're here. Save him."

An old guy was standing there, all shriveled up in a long, black wool coat. He was grinning at me. A big, grey, toothless grin. Not a tooth in his head, his face sunk in over his gums. It was strange, but in a way, it looked good on him. I mean, it was kind of disarming. With a dark blue cap rolled up tight above his ears, he appeared to be completely bald. He looked like Jacques Cousteau, in a way.

He quit grinning at me and instead turned to grin up at the poor bastard hanging out over the railroad tracks.

It made me dizzy, just to look up at him through the webbing. The steel braces formed sort of a diamond pattern against the sky. Big clouds were floating by, and it seemed as though the whole bridge itself was moving. He wasn't struggling much anymore, just kind of hanging on. He made another attempt at swinging his leg up, but hardly got it much higher than his waist. Then he just swung back and forth, hanging limp.

It was unbearable. Any moment, I expected him to drop. There wasn't a damn thing to do, either. Just stand stand there on the edge of the bank and watch him, the poor bastard. It's crazy, but suddenly I didn't know what to do with my hands. I was scratching and sniffling and stuffing them in my pockets. It was crazy, but I didn't know what to do with them. So I cupped them around my mouth and yelled the first thing that popped into my head. "911."

It was the cruelest thing I've ever done. The poor white bastard looked at me with such hope, it was devastating. For I had nothing else to offer him. But he was relying on me. If I showed despair, he was going to drop fifty feet onto the railroad tracks. There would be time to think in fifty feet. Not much, but it'd be terrible. With my hands still cupped around my mouth, I yelled again.

"Don't panic."

"Pretty damn demanding, aren't you?"

It was the old guy, Joe, grinning at me; all grey stubble and wrinkles and he's grinning at me like I'd just made an ass of myself, but it doesn't matter. Lunatics and crazy bastards. I yelled again.

"Hang on."

The poor bastard was snarling at me. Joe snorted.

"Now that's the soundest advice I've heard in years." Joe nodded his head in sombre agreement, looking mockingly serious. I resented the hell out of it. "Then you save him, if you're so damn smart," I said, placing my hands ridiculously on my hips. Joe grinned like he had me. Then he yelled over his shoulder at the poor guy.

"You fall, don't land on them eggs. You're liable to break one."

It hit like the crack of a whip. His body tensed. One foot began to come up, twitching a few times, then plunging skyward up to the steel beam, his toes clamoring frantically for a moment, before slipping and dropping dramatically downward, swinging him for the last of his strength.

"Sling the sack over your back and fall forward," Joe yelled, scratching his crotch with pure pleasure.

The poor bastard let loose this wild, insane animal cry of frustration and anger, throwing his foot skyward one last time and hooking a toe. He paused, then slowly the next toe climbed up, and one by one the others followed, bringing the foot, hooking an ankle. Then the knee was hooked and slowly he pulled himself up onto the beam, lying motionless, face down flat and hugging the steel.

Joe cupped his hands and yelled in a real dead way, sounding surprisingly like me.

"Now, be careful."

Then he started snorting and cackling and gripping his side, laughing at everything I and everyone else had ever done. It was stupid, but I resented it, still thinking pride was valuable, since it was all I had. Refusing to smile. Insisting that what we'd just witnessed was not a laughing matter. Scowling, I waited out Joe's humor, which required patience. Joe could be irritating at times. When he finally did quit laughing, he took a look at me, from my suitcase to the corduroy suit to the stony look on my face, then started all over again.

"You selling Amway, son? You got something that takes shit out of shorts?

If so, my friend here would be an easy sale." Then he yelled up at Caeser.

"Caeser! Amway guy's here. How much shitty shorts cleaner should I order?"

Caeser lifted his head and let loose a string of vicious threats, scattering a cloud of pigeons from the bracing around him. Joe chuckled, obviously enjoying himself, then looked level at me.

"Say, you retarded or something?"

I should have said 'maybe' in a real dark voice and given him a blank stare, instead of blurting out 'no.' Miserable, I lit a cigarette and blew smoke. "Easy, son," Joe said soothingly, as though talking to a child. Then he smiled real friendly. "Say, you got anymore smokes?"

"Maybe," I said, in a dark, menacing voice. My timing was way off. Joe just smiled, humoring me.

"That's good. That's real good. Guy don't wanna tip his hand and spill the beans, you know. Guy can't be too careful out here. Never know who he's going to run into. A bird in the hand is worth two in the bush. Hell, worth more than that. Three, four in the bush. But I ain't telling you nothing. Obvious that you know how to take care of yourself. The reason I asked at all is that I seen you were smoking and it's been awhile since I've known the pleasure."

He was talking to me as though to a child.

"What the hell do birds have to do with smokes?" I asked, not trying to hide the disgust in my voice. "It's the dumbest analogy I've ever heard."

Joe smiled. "You're right. You're God damn right. It was stupid. But now, I ain't claiming intelligence. Hell no, if I was intelligent, I sure as hell wouldn't be down here collecting pigeon eggs with a one-eyed pirate like him." He looked up at Caeser. Caeser hadn't yet moved, still laying face down on the beam, bear hugging it.

"You bringing them eggs down?" Joe yelled. "Getting damn late for breakfast. You know how it upsets my stomach to miss breakfast."

Caeser lifted his head and let loose another string of curses, causing more pigeons to scatter nervously. Joe smiled at me.

"Look, you hungry? Caeser ever makes it down, we'll have scrambled eggs and potatoes. Even have an onion and some ketchup, if you're interested. How does a good breakfast sound? Trade you for a couple smokes.

Hell, we even have coffee."

I had the extra smokes. A whole suitcase full. And I was hungry. Scrambled eggs and ketchup sounded good. Still, I felt a need to be cagey.

"How many smokes?"

Joe's eyes narrowed for just a second, then he caught himself and resumed his wide open, honest look.

"Why, I don't know. Sure as hell hate to take a man's last cigarette off him. A man's pleasures are few out here, and Lord knows they're far between. A man gets to where he starts counting his smokes, and that's a man facing a low, rough stretch. I'll be damned if I'll hasten a man's descent. You counting your smokes, son, you best hang onto them. You're welcomed to breakfast, though. Never let it be said that Joe and Caeser would deprive a hungry man a meal just because he's running out of smokes. It would be an un-Christian thing to do. There but for the grace of God go I, you know."

I was sensitive to pity. The fact that both the mayor and Joe were quoting scriptures, the same scriptures, magnified my reaction.

"I'm not saying I'm counting smokes. I just want to know how many you want in exchange for breakfast."

Joe acted concerned.

"Easy, son. Don't let your pride trip you into giving away the last of your smokes. Nothing like a man's pride to hasten his own descent into hell. No, man, keep your smokes. Breakfast is free."

Somehow, I felt compelled to prove my worth in cigarettes, as though they were an indication of my spiritual well being.

"Dammit, I don't want a free breakfast. I'm hungry and I've got the means to pay."

"Ok," Joe raised his hands in defeat. "You're a proud man. Some men are strong enough to be proud. Others are stupid enough, and the rest are just damn lucky. I'm not sure into which category you fit, but now, I've got my principles, see? And that's all I've got, and if I sacrifice my principles I ain't got nothing. You see what I'm saying? You force a man like me, destitute and spiritually exhausted, to sacrifice my principles, and I'm finished. Nothing left to hang onto. Condemned to the vast expanses of emptiness, adrift in my own form of madness. Man, can't you see that I'm cornered? I can't let you pay for breakfast, not without assuring my own sense of morality that you can afford it, and therefore aren't hastening your own demise because of a foolish sense of pride."

Joe looked at me in an earnest, almost desperate way, as though he were close to tears, caught in his dilemma. I was naive, and let the bird slip free, spilling the beans.

"Dammit, I've got half a pack in my pocket and fifteen more right here in my suitcase."

Joe looked surprised, then skeptical, then sympathetic. "Easy, son. Half a pack ain't nothing to be ashamed of."

Infuriated, I slammed the suitcase down on the ground between us, snapped it open and yanked back my greens, exposing my wealth of cigarettes. Contemptuously, I grabbed a pack and tossed it at Joe, flinging it carelesssly into the weeds, expecting him to scurry after it like a starving man after a piece of bread. Instead, Joe reached out and snatched it out of the air, with one hand, quick as a blink, like Hank chasing a fly. He was damn near as fast as Hank.

"I'll be damned," he said, giving me a wink and a grin. He looked down at the suitcase, and I became self-conscious of my greens, stuffing them back in and slamming the suitcase shut. Joe laughed, shaking his head, yelling up at Caeser.

"Get your ass down here, we've got a paying customer for breakfast."

Caeser threw a few token curses down at him, then started moving slowly through the bracing, threading his way carefully. Caeser had to move slow, on account of his depth perception being off. He was missing an eye.

Joe headed up the riverbank on a path overgrown with willow saplings, their new spring leaves shining green and tender. The path led up to the base of the bridge, where it struck the west bank and became Brewery Street. A camp was nestled in the cool shadows under the bridgedeck, next to the massive concrete footing. Two big rocks, about five feet high, a red one and a blue one, were spaced fifteen feet apart, with a fire ring, a couple of chairs, and a blue Coleman cooler hidden between them. The chairs sat on either side of the fire. One was an old Morris recliner, a wooden frame with two brown sofa cushions for comfort. The other was a tattered red stuffed chair, with three legs and a rock. The seat straps were broken, and there was a guy sunk deep in it, reading a newspaper, his head and shoulders sticking up just past the tattered arms. Joe sighed when he saw the guy sitting there, mumbling something about crazy people.

His name was Charles, and he looked up when he heard Joe mumbling. He was maybe in his fifties, with greying hair, curly and clipped short. He wore a beard, groomed and frosted along his jaws. The smell of Old Spice aftershave permeated the air around him. Round, thick, wire rimmed glasses magnified his intensely focused eyes and their impact. He spoke forcefully with indignation.

"You won't believe it," he declared as we approached the fire ring. "You just won't believe it."

He was talking about something he'd read in the paper. When he spoke, he held out the paper, shaking it at Joe. Joe sighed and poured us each a cup of coffee from the pot simmering beside the fire. Charles already had a cup, balancing on the arm of his chair.

"What's wrong now, Charles?" Joe finally asked in a tired voice. "What's wrong?" Charles exclaimed, waving the paper. "I'll tell you

what's wrong! Greed and political scandal! The masses are being condemned to misery for the benefit of a few elitists!"

Joe chuckled.

"Same as last week, I believe."

Charles leaned forward excitedly, pushing his glasses up his nose.

"No. Yes. Maybe it's the same, in a way. But this is more immediate. You know what they want to do down at the power plant? You know what them short-sighted, money grabbing bastards want to do now? They want to store their nuclear waste in dry casks, right on the riverbank. Can you believe it? Just a day's walk down the river, Joe, they want to store their nuclear poison, enough poison to contaminate the largest watershed in the entire nation. Right on the banks of the damn river!"

Joe had taken off a shoe and was trying to shake something out of it, reaching his fingers inside and giving it his undivided attention. So Charles turned to me. I'd been watching him with interest. Another dysfunctional. The place was crawling with them. Some sort of hyperactive neural disorder. The veins bulged on his neck and forehead as his blood pressure shot up. His eyes were amplified by his glasses, and when he looked at me I was struck by their intensity.

"Right on the banks of the river," he repeated.

"Who wants to put it there?" I asked, though I really didn't want to get involved. He was intense.

"The people who own the God damn power plant. Them and their politicians, the ones they helped get elected!" He was shouting at me, his eyes bulging in the lenses of his glasses. Then he stopped short, and looked at me, as though noticing me for the first time.

"I don't believe we've met," he said in a cordial tone. "My name's Charles." "Emerson," I answered, getting up to shake his hand. He had on so much aftershave my eyes watered. Not that using Old Spice would indicate a dysfunctional personality, but he must have been wearing half a bottle. He fished a pack of cigarettes from his shirt pocket and lit a smoke, nodding at my suitcase.

"Where you headed?"

I just shrugged my shoulders. "Not my suitcase," I said, kind of hoping he thought I stole it. I was feeling insecure.

"Say, Charles," Joe had slipped his shoe back on and was looking humble. "You wouldn't have an extra smoke, would you? Damn, that's fresh smelling tobacco. What the hell brand is it?"

Charles pulled out a crumpled pack of Eagles and tapped one out for Joe.

Joe was the sneakiest bastard I've ever met.

"Generic? Well, I'll be damned. But then, it's

been awhile since I've known the pleasure. Coffee and cigarettes and scrambled eggs. Yes sir, it's a fine morning. You hungry, Charles?"

A big truck rolled across the bridge, its engine roaring loud. The storm grates jumped and rattled, the sound echoing under the bridge, cavelike. The massive concrete footing was covered with graffitti; names and dates, poetry and profanity. Cigarette butts lay scattered in the sand and broken glass littered the fire ring. Still, there was a sense of order about the place. A sort of balance between permanence and transience.

Joe and Charles paid little attention to Caeser moving through the beams and braces overhead. They seemed not to care. I kept watching, though, expecting him to slip. He looked like a giant spider, long arms and legs, crawling across a web of steel. His movements were deliberate. The pigeon nests were cradled in the crotches of the diagonal bracing and tucked up under the bridge deck, on the I-beam infrastructure. The nests were thick, and Caeser paused often to fill the egg sack. The birds fluttered around nervously, but apparently had not formed too deep an attachment to their eggs, for none attacked him.

It took him over an hour to work his way back to the west end of the bridge. As the bridge approached the bank, the clearance was reduced to a mere fifteen feet. Still, Caeser moved slowly. Only when he had properly secured his next handhold would he move his body forward, then pause to secure the next.

"How are they laying?" Joe asked casually, looking up as Caeser reached the top of the concrete footing behind us.

"Like the greatest flock of pigeons in the world!" Caeser exclaimed.

Charles snorted, hiding behind the newspaper.

A thick rope hung down the face of the footing. Caeser repelled down, his bare feet not slipping on the smooth concrete. He seemed to use his toes as well as his fingers.

"I have returned," he announced, taking a deep bow, his head of tangled hair hanging everywhere. His beard was thick and scruffy, and I swear there were pieces of dry grass in it.

"Caeser," Joe said, "that was very close. I'll scramble the eggs, you need only harvest them."

With a laugh bordering on hysteria, Caeser handed the sack of eggs to Joe. He walked bull-legged and stiff. I assumed he'd strained something in his struggle for survival. With his one eye, he looked at me through crazy hair. It was disconcerting. The last thing I felt like was a menace to anything. I'm not kidding, Caeser was the wildest looking crazy bastard I've ever met. He held out his hand.

"Name's Caeser, mister. Caeser, Pigeon Master. Pigeonist Extraordinaire. Keeper of the Flock. The greatest flock of birds in the city. Hell, in the state. Dammit man, this could be the greatest flock of pigeons in the entire world." He raised his arms, long, sinewy arms with huge, bony fists, over his head, and from deep in his throat, began cooing like a pigeon, throwing his insane call down across the valley. Clouds of birds swirled through the bridge webbing and down over the railroad tracks, swarming toward and back from the loading docks. None acknowledged Caeser's crazy cooing, but it was unsettling as hell. I had no idea how to respond. Charles was sunk deep in his chair, engrossed in the newspaper he held in front of his face. Joe was smoking a cigarette, his other shoe off, examining his toes through a hole in his sock. Neither seemed to notice Caeser's blatant display of insanity, or consider it odd.

"Emerson," I said, as Caeser shook my hand.

"Glad to meet you, Mr Emerson." He nodded at the suitcase. "Where you headed?"

"Not his suitcase," Joe answered. "You want to keep any of these eggs to sell?"

"Keep a dozen," Caeser said, "Promised Murphy he'd get some this week. Been bugging the hell out of me. Now, Mr Emerson, if you'll excuse me, I'll be going down to the river to rinse my shorts. Although a Master Pigeonist, I have yet to master the art of flying. The acrobatics you witnessed this morning were unintentional and, frankly, scared the shit out of me."

Caeser waddled off bull-legged down the path, disappearing into the willows above the railroad tracks. Joe counted out a dozen eggs and placed them in a nest he scooped out beside the blue rock. One by one, he began to crack the remaining pile, dripping the yoke and muck into a blackened frying pan. Charles muttered from behind the newspaper.

Suddenly, there was a barking of dogs and a rabbit raced out of the brush south of the camp, circled back, and disappeared an instant before Alice burst into the clearing, followed by Sadie and Clyde. They ran in circles, noses to the ground and tails in the air, butting heads. Franklin stepped out of the brush and started cussing them.

"You damn morons," and the dogs bounced around him, wagging their tails and looking happy.

"If you're looking for breakfast, it'll be a small portion. We've already got two guests, counting Charles. Birds are laying good, but five helpings is going to strain it."

Franklin held up a coffee can.

"Already ate," he said to Joe, "You ever taste possum? Brought some stew over. Possum's not that bad. Taste's like pork, in a way. Hello, son. Fine day to be alive, won't you agree?"

I just shrugged my shoulders, digging out the last of my change and settling up with Franklin as well as possible, promising to make good on the rest when I got the chance. He accepted the sixty cents with a gracious bow. "For the sake of my white companion, I thank you for your honesty," he replied.

Joe was watching us closely.

"Is that why you're scratching? You got fleas, son?"

I just kind of shrugged. It's not something a person readily admits. "Dammit," Joe said, "Dammit all to hell. Fleas ain't healthy, son." He

looked at me as though I'd aquired a bad habit. Franklin waved him off. "Hell, fleas won't kill you. Here, check out the stew."

Both Charles and Joe were impressed with the stew, sampling it from the coffee can, and decided to add it to the eggs. The whole mess was simmering over the fire. Actually, it smelled pretty good. I hadn't eaten in twenty-four hours, except for the stale sweetroll.

Caeser returned with clean, wet pants and a clutch of chives he'd snatched on the way. He crushed them in his hands and sprinkled it over the eggs and possum. Charles was explaining the nuclear waste storage proposal to Franklin, and Caeser began to ridicule him.

"Dammit, Charles, you're over reacting again."

"Over reacting? It's a scandal!" Charles' blood pressure was building again, his veins bulging and pulsating. "Do you have any concept of what a nuclear spill into the river would mean?"

Franklin began theorizing about the effects of radioactive gene mutation on the evolutionary process. Joe sighed, stirring the eggs, which were beginning to coagulate. I just sat there, smoking like an idiot and feeling out of place.

"And it's not even on the front page! Lookit this. They've got a picture of Mckinnley shaking hands with the regional director of the National Dental Association."

It was the same paper I'd seen plastered to the concrete floor of the bus shelter the day before.

"He's running for Congress," Charles was shaking the paper at us, "And you know what his platform is based on? Cavities! They're going to build a nuclear waste dump on the banks of the greatest watershed in the nation, and our mayor is worried about how many cavities his constituents have." Charles threw down the paper in disgust.

"Say, I was talking to the mayor this morning," Franklin said. "And he did seem interested in my teeth. Ain't that right, son?"

I resented him calling me son again, but no one else seemed to notice. They were all interested in the mayor dropping in on me and Franklin earlier that morning. Franklin explained how the mayor had surprised us, showing up with tv cameras and shaking our hands.

"Must be some kind of crusade," he concluded.

They were impressed. The eggs singed while Joe sat listening, and he cursed, scraping them off the pan. Charles shook his head, muttering to himself. Caeser looked thoughtful, running his fingers through his beard.

"Boys," he said, "looks like we've become fashionable."

Joe smiled his toothless grin and scooped the eggs and possum onto some plastic plates, the word Frisbee embossed on the bottom of mine. Franklin wasn't hungry, but his dogs were. While we were talking, they ate half the eggs Caeser was going to sell to Murphy. Joe got up cursing and tried to kick Alice. Franklin took offense and called Joe a careless bastard for setting the eggs where the dogs could find them. "It's instincts, dammit, you can't fault them." And the two of them were arguing when Charles stood up in disgust and called everyone an idiot for worrying about cavities and pigeon eggs when we were on the brink of a nuclear disaster, and Caeser took offense to that and called Charles an alarmist.

Disgusted, Charles walked off, headed north past the red rock, the newspaper clenched angrily in his hand. Offended, Franklin headed south, past the blue rock, with his coffee can, the three dogs bouncing through the weeds around him. A diesel came across the bridge, downshifting with a roar, rattling storm grates and shaking loose a cloud of pigeons which swarmed down over the railroad tracks and out over the river.

Joe was a thief. He occasionally picked a pocket, but his main line of work was shoplifting fruit and canned goods from the SuperValue on Sixth Street. A can of tuna went for four smokes, an apple sold for two- to start out with. Caeser provided me with a couple of blankets for fifteen smokes apiece. They were good blankets, heavy and clean, and the only time I ever came out ahead on a deal made under the bridge.

It was obvious from the start they let me stick around because of my cigarettes. In a way, Ron did me a favor by blowing my money on smokes. It gave me a measure of wealth, providing Joe and Caeser with instant gratification for any services provided. With pigeon eggs, tuna and apples, my diet was healthy enough. Indeed, Joe and Ceaser seemed to thrive on it. None the less, I became sick.

In the end, the cigarettes worked against me. They provided a false sense of security, allowing me to embrace my apathy. I simply withdrew further, rolling up in my blankets. I spoke to no one, except to barter with Joe and Caeser. My apathy developed, uninhibited and on fertile ground, blossoming into lethargy. Twelve, fifteen hours a day I rolled up in my blankets, emerging only to eat and then to go sit down on the bluffs and watch the pigeons swarming over the loading docks. My disorientation deepened. I realized my dilemma, but whenever I focused long enough to complete a thought pattern, despair was inevitably the result. A deep, gut wrenching despair.

It must have been May, maybe part of June. Time blurred. My feet kicked out and I'm slipping, trying to grab onto something, but there's nothing there. Nothing but a bunch of bums. Losers. They're not going to catch me. They'll help me up. They'll be there when I hit, and they'll pick up the pieces, keep a few for themselves; set me up mostly straight. But they're just watching now, see me coming down out of control, making sure they're out of the way when I hit. They can't catch me. I'm coming too fast. Only a fool would try. That's the thing about those bums: They're nobody's fool. In their eyes, I was simply a cigarette dispenser. As my supply began to run low, I began to resent the situation.

Joe raised the price of tuna to six smokes, and all fruit was now a solid four, over-ripe bananas included. I resented the hell out of it. Bums are no better than anybody else. They're lazy and greedy and sneaky, just like everybody else.

Falling through a haze, desperately detached. Buzzed. Hypnotized by the buzzing of my overloaded nervous system, gridlocked in a desperate attempt at self-preservation. A fragile equilibrium of denial and despair, an hypnotically induced paralysis of the mind. Thought bound. One moment away from redemption or complete breakdown. Building resonance, the buzz increased, feeding on itself, running along my nerves, washing over and obliterating all reason, rising to the heightened state of sustained anxiety, reverberating to the point of mental fatigue. Blessed fatigue. Too tired to give a damn. Letting go, falling backwards, riding down on the sustaining buzz of apathy. Just a sick feeling in my guts and a vague sense that things are going to get worse. Joe raised the price of tuna to ten smokes. I had less than two packs left.

I refused to pay ten smokes. I argued, protesting against his greed. Called him a thief and a bastard. Cursed the living hell out of him. All to no avail. Joe simply ate the tuna himself. Right in front of me. Chewing it with his fingers, rolling it into a pulp, sucking the juices, tearing it into little bits which he held in his mouth until they were soft enough to swallow, gumming patiently. Joe was the slowest eater I've ever seen.

I was outraged. Out of my mind. Fleas were tearing my flesh apart. My body was raw and bleeding from flea bites and frustrated scratching, and I was exhausted with frustration.

I decided to die. I wrapped myself in my blankets, my own damn blankets, and laid down behind the red rock.

Joe and Caeser didn't seem to care. They didn't seem to notice. It drove Charles nuts, though. Charles was a crazy bastard anyways. Mad as hell.

The picture of Franklin and myself with the Mayor made the front page of the newspaper. It was pathetic. With a constipated scowl, I'm glaring ridiculously at the camera, hands folded passively over my crotch. Franklin looks like he's about to be awarded a medal, stiff with pride, and the mayor is holding the goatskull, beaming with the self-satisfaction of the philanthropist. In the background, poor Sadie is dragging herself across the ground, a strained look on her face. Right below it, the caption read:

Mental Illness and Tooth Decay: Is there a connection?

I didn't give a damn, but it was embarrassing as hell and I resented it anyways. And I resented Charles, who brought the paper over to show Joe and Caeser, who thought it was funny as hell. They worked a smoke off him while Charles ranted about me being part of a conspiracy.

The reason I was lying behind the rock had nothing to do with Charles. It was absolutely none of his damn business. The son of a bitch wouldn't leave me alone, though. He thought I was acting like a victim. He thought I liked being a victim because it got me attention. He thought I liked attention because I'd gotten my picture on the front page of the God damn newspaper with the mayor. And he was mad about all the attention I was getting because there were more important things to worry about, like storing nuclear waste on the riverbank. He thought I thought my personal crisis was more important than the welfare of future generations. And he was right. I did not give a damn about nuclear waste, lying there scratching fleas and sweating and trying to die, sick as all hell. Raw with flea bites and stinking with perspiration and so sore from lying on the rocky ground it hurt to move.

It infuriated him. He'd been over nearly every day since the picture had been published, ranting about it, expecting me to apologize or something.

It infuriated me. The son of a bitch wouldn't leave me alone. I refused to renounce my victim status. I would die first, becoming the ultimate victim just to spite him. Charles could be aggravating, though. He taunted me.

They're sitting around the fire, Charles ranting at Joe and Caeser. I can't see him because I'm rolled up behind the rock, but I know he's waving the stupid picture around. And he's talking like I'm not even there, or he doesn't care whether I hear or not. "What in the hell is so important about his damn teeth? They're going to store nuclear waste on the banks of the greatest river in the nation, and the mayor's worried about his teeth. When he don't give enough of a damn to even brush them, just laying there like a victim."

"Ah, leave the kid alone," I heard Caeser say, "Christ, Charles, it ain't his fault. Probably just miserable with hormones. Won't let him think straight. You remember about hormones, don't you Charles?"

I resented the hell out of Caeser discussing my hormones with a crazy bastard like Charles, right in front of me as though neither cared if I heard or not.

"Oh, that's it," Charles was shouting. "The poor kid needs to get laid, and we're all suppose to feel sorry for him. Laying there like the first person who's ever felt it. A damn victim, that's what he is. A damn hormonal fucking victim."

Charles was rustling his paper and I heard him leaving, coming around the red rock. I was scratching fleas and miserable and mad as hell, but I knew my apathy was driving Charles crazy, and refused to give him the satisfaction of knowing that I gave a damn about anything the crazy bastard thought.

"A damn hormonal fucking victim," he shouted as he walked past and spit on the ground. I heard it hit, not three feet from my head, I heard his spit strike a rock with a wet sound. I was too surprised to do anything, and Charles was already gone before I'd made up my mind.

I lay listening to the traffic crossing the bridge overhead. It was late morning, the sun was already high over the valley. I'd been lying there for fifteen hours or more, rolled up behind the rock, away from the fire. My body ached from the hard ground and the fleas were chewing me raw, and I stunk.

Joe was talking now.

"Things ain't right," he said in kind of a thoughtful voice, for Joe, loud enough for me to hear. "Things just ain't right. Something's out of balance. Things just don't feel right to me, somehow," he concluded.

Caeser laughed.

"Nothing's right when Charles is around. I'm telling you, the man's driving himself crazy. You know what Charles needs?"

Joe didn't answer the question.

"It ain't Charles," he said, "It's the kid. He ain't healthy. Crawling with fleas and moping around like he's ready to die. It ain't right. Something's gotta change. The kid's gotta snap out of it."

Joe wasn't worried about me listening. He talked about me as though it didn't matter if I heard or not, as though I were just an idiot, lying there because I liked it. Again, in his own way, Caeser tried to defend me.

"It ain't the kid's fault. I bet it's hormones. The kid's probably still a virgin, for crying out loud. Think about it, Joe, the kid's young."

Lying there listening to those two old bastards talk about me like I was just a kid with a hormone problem started something stirring. Out of the ashes, the spark glowed, flickered, then glowed again. I got to my feet, feeling sore and dangerous.

There was a can of tuna fish sitting on a rock beside Joe, a can of tuna fish and an orange. I indicated to Joe that I was hungry, defiantly scratching myself. It's none of his damn business if I've got fleas. It's no concern of his or anyone else's.

I stood scratching and tapping out smokes for the old bum. Disdainfully. They were my damn smokes. He weren't no God damn better than me, just a misfitted, shoplifting, toothless bum. Joe's eyes flashed. Just for a second, but I caught it. Then he looked bored, and reached out with a stick, poking at the fire. I held forward fourteen smokes, the going rate for a can of tuna and an orange.

Joe just poked kinda lazy at the fire, then spoke in a bored voice. "Prices've gone up. Pack for the tuna. Half a pack for the orange."

He didn't even look up. He just looked bored, poking at the fire with his stick, like he didn't give a damn what I thought about it.

From the ashes of my self-pity, the spark glowed bright, sending up a little wisp of smoke.

I was disgusted with everything. With myself,

mostly, but I transposed my disgust onto Joe, and the damn fleas eating me alive, and the empty feeling in my guts and the ache in my muscles and the hopeless, worthless situation I'd found myself in and the despair that was tearing me apart, and the old bastard was pushing. He didn't even look up. Pack of smokes for a God damn can of tuna. I wasn't a fool. No longer was I going to just lie there, like a helpless victim, and let crazy bastards spit on me.

"Easy, son," Caeser said, sensing my anger beginning to burn. But he wasn't trying to calm me. He was warning me, warning me to back off and take whatever shit the world wanted to throw at me because I was in no position to argue.

My mind began to tilt. I felt a lifting wave and thought I was going to pass out. But across the emptiness, all I could see, the only thing I had was some anger and a little pride. Desperation gripped my guts hard, and I had to do something.

"You bastard," I growled, and charged. Joe was still sitting there bored, like I wasn't anything to worry about, poking at the fire like he didn't give a damn about what I thought or even did.

One more step, and I would've busted his neck.

He was just sitting there, that bony head on that skinny neck and my forearm was poised and ready to smash him, and then he ducked and I missed and he's coming up underneath me and I'm sailing over the chair, over the cooler, slamming onto the rocky ground twelve feet away, flat on my back and Joe's got hold of my hair and a knee in my throat and he's ready to shove that burning stick straight up my nose. And his eyes are telling me he'll do it.

One move, and he'll do it.

The glow off that stick was hot in my face; the smell of smoke burning close. Pointed right up my nose.

"Easy," Caeser said, but I'm not sure if he's talking to me or not. It sounds like he's still in his chair and I don't say anything. The stick was burning hot.

Joe just kept the pressure steady. We stared at one another.

"Son," he finally said, his eyes not leaving mine, "The price of tuna's gone up. It's called a cost of living increase. You ain't gotta pay it, and I'm not going to make you. But if you want it, you pay my price. Now, I'm getting tired of you moping around here like you're trapped and we owe it to you. You're not, and we don't. You understand that, and you're welcomed to stay. You don't wanna live, you go somewhere else to die. But if you stay, you're gonna start trying to live. It's damn hard enough without watching someone else not even try."

"Easy, Joe," Caeser was saying, "Don't burn him, for crying out loud."

My lip was getting scorched. My whole face burned with humiliation. It was humiliating. There wasn't any more anger left, just humiliation burning me up inside. Joe sensed it and let me go. He stood up, still holding the stick, and held out his hand. I couldn't even say anything, just took his hand and let him help me up. I had no more fight, and he knew it. Caeser knew it, too. There was an awkward moment when Joe sat back in his chair and I took a seat on the cooler. Caeser spoke to ease the tension.

"Well now, if you boys have reached some sort of understanding, perhaps now we can turn our thoughts toward solving some of the world's more pressing problems."

Joe was poking at the fire again.

"One more thing, first," he said, not mean, but you could tell he was still serious. "Before we solve the world's problems, we gotta take care of our own."

Caeser chuckled.

"Old man, you're getting damn ornery in your later years, and it's making you a demanding son of a bitch. What's eating you now?"

Caeser was starting to enjoy himself. He sensed the crisis had passed. I wasn't so sure. I just sat there, half in a buzz. My pride was in remission, my anger cooled. I just wasn't sure of anything.

"Nothing," Joe answered, "and I want to keep it that way. The kid's crawling with fleas, and it's making him miserable. Fleas ain't healthy. They'll drive a man crazy."

Joe spoke of me to Caeser as though I wasn't there. Then he waited for me to answer. Another awkward silence followed, only this time Caeser didn't say anything to get me off the hook. It was my choice. I could leave, or I could stay. But if I stayed, it would be on their terms. Joe poked at the fire. Caeser didn't say anything.

"What the hell am I suppose to do about them, for Christ' sake?" I decided to stay. Fleas are miserable.

Caeser chuckled. He knew the cure for fleas.

Shadows lay deep in the valley. The lights from the city push back the darkness which condenses down in the ravines and sneaks out across the railyard, crouching beneath the lines of boxcars left overnight on the side tracks. Like black holes, the shadows swallow you up: an oasis of cover in the bright light washing over the floodplain. Huge lights, high on thick poles that hum and buzz and the moths circle in thick clouds. A cat slinks across the tracks, mouse dangling limp in its mouth, then stops, staring at the shadows beneath the boxcars. It can't see us, but it knows we're there and stares before trotting off with its belly down low to the ground.

I was following Joe across the flat expanse of the railyard, trying to stay hidden in the shadows. Dressed in a pair of my greens and carrying a length of rope, I was having trepidations about my choice to stay. Joe was adamant about ridding me of fleas, though. He was trying to reassure me that it was for the benefit of everyone concerned.

But why, I wanted to know, could this not wait until morning, when the sun was shining and the whole ordeal would seem less threatening?

"Certain aspects of the vagrant lifestyle must be conducted under the cover of darkness," he replied. "Besides, fleas ain't healthy, and the sooner you're rid of them, the better."

We waited in the shadow of a line of boxcars. Joe was nervous about security. We weren't breaking the law, except for maybe trespassing I suppose, but Joe didn't trust the security guards who cruised the yard in blue cars, flashlights poking into the shadows. They're usually drunk by now, he says, but if they catch you they'll have a laugh at your expense.

I didn't know what he meant, but I followed close and ran when he told me to.

The yard was all lit up, but near the river, up north of the docks, the riverbank was deep in shadows. Here the bank was a smooth, solid concrete wall about six feet above the black, slow moving surface of the river. It was dark and hard to see, but the power could be felt. Slow and black and dredged deep for barge traffic.

Standing there, stark naked, holding onto the rope, I felt unsure of everything. My trust had been placed with Joe and Caeser. Desperately, I tried to re-center myself, trying to be reassuring.

Caeser was back at camp, disinfecting my clothes and blankets in a pot of boiling water while I was to bathe in the river for fifteen minutes, with nothing but the rope wrapped around my waist and the plastic straw to breathe through.

"You gotta keep your head under as much as you can," Joe was telling me as I tied the rope around my waist and he secured the other end to a barge anchor, a heavy hook of steel embedded in the concrete. "Breathe through the straw and wiggle around as much as you can to shake the bastards loose. And don't panic. Fifteen minutes is going to seem like a long time. A damn long time. You're going to think I'm gone and left you to drown. But I ain't. I'll be up here counting, so don't panic and yell. Them barge bastards hear you, they'll come running to haul your ass out. Voices carry over the water at night. They'll hear you and call security and then I will be gone, you can bet. Just lie there and wait."

I stood on the concrete wall another minute, feeling the power of the river below, watching the lights of a tug working off the loading docks. A spotlight swept across the water, and before I could move, passed over us.

"Better go, son," Joe said, almost like he was sorry. "They can't see us this far, but no use waiting for trouble. I'll count. You just lie there and wait and I'll yank hard when it's been fifteen minutes."

I felt trapped. The whole damn mess seemed to have me trapped. Then I realized Joe was right, in a way. No one was making me jump. It was my choice.

I said the hell with it, and jumped.

The water was cold, the current strong, and underwater the tug engines hummed in my ears with a pressure that seemed about to smother me. The first thing I did was forget about the damn straw. The current pulled heavy and the rope swung me in close to the wall and the water rushed over me and I shook my head free, trying not to drown. I panicked like hell, figuring Joe was trying to drown me. The bastard had tricked me and was going to let me drown. I tried controlling my thoughts, counting the seconds, but this made the minutes seem ridiculously long. My imagination raced. At that moment, Caeser was probably going through my suitcase, dividing up the remaining cigarettes and clean socks between him and Joe, keeping an extra pair or two out of the deal. I swallowed and coughed up water and was getting tired and in my mind I cussed the living hell out of Joe, who was probably just sitting up there, smoking and waiting for me to give up before he cut the line. Just as I was about to start yelling like holy hell, Joe yanked on the rope and helped me up.

It was exhausting, but lying there on the bank, a good feeling came to me. My teeth were chattering, but Joe wrapped me in a clean blanket. My body, raw from flea bites, felt clean and refreshed. I could detect no flea activity whatsoever, though I monitored myself closely as we ran, waited, dodged between the boxcars and climbed the path back to camp.

As promised, Caeser had boiled my clothes clean and they were draped over the rocks, already almost dry. Digging through my suitcase, under pretense of looking for my toothbrush, I counted my smokes and socks and they were all there. After brushing my teeth, I just sat around and listened to Joe and Caeser lie and argue. The storm grates rattled with the traffic passing overhead and the pigeons stirred restlessly, making watery sounds up in the shadows of the girders.

I was starting to feel better.

I'm not making excuses for becoming a vagrant. That would imply regret. It was not a regretful experience. It was humiliating at worse, humbling at best. I was given choices. Having chosen to stay, I soon had to choose between eating and going hungry.

In a way, Joe did me a favor by stealing my cigarettes. I was forced to surrender my apathy. If I wanted to eat, that is.

I was assigned the task of providing wood for the fire. It was the first real responsibility of my life. It may seem laughable to the institutionalized person, who does not have to gather fuel in order to eat. Unencumbered by the necessity of tending a fire, one's thoughts are presumably liberated to pursue loftier concepts. This may be true. I won't argue about it. All I know is that while searching the valley for firewood, hatchet in hand, daydreaming on the bluffs of the river in the warm sunshine of a midsummer day, I began to wonder.

Where the hell did all the water come from? I pondered this. I thought about walking up the river someday to find out. I wondered how far I'd have to go. I wondered if I could. I mean, if people would just let me walk along the river for as far as I wanted, or if there was some place I'd have to stop because there was a fence or something. I wondered who'd build a fence like that, and what was on the other side.

Instincts stirred. Instincts buried beneath the numbing boredom of the institution began to awaken. My senses sharpened, and began to focus. Although I lacked the ability to decipher meaning, I felt something. Something way down inside.

The sound of owls late at night, talking and laughing along the bluffs; an eery, wild sound. Something sneaking around in the shadows. And thunder. The crack and roll down the valley, so fierce it made me curl up next to the rock, wrapped in my blankets, the spray of rain on a gust of wind and the willows thrashing in the flashes of lightning. The power of it ran along my nerves and left me dazed and when the rain fell so thick, it was mesmerizing. Down between the rocks and the fire's burning warm and there's enough wood to last all night, if we want to stay up. I can't really explain it. It just felt good.

Waking up beneath the bridge always came as something of a surprise to me, though. It was the weak link between my previous identity and my new one. Almost like starting my transition to vagrancy over again every morning. For I was not a true bum. I was a product of the institution, attuned to time and order. My life was based on a schedule. Through the night, my internal time clock readjusted itself. I woke up hungry and disoriented, stiff and sore, diesels roaring overhead and the smell of woodsmoke drifting low. At Heartsfield, breakfast was served at 7:30, lunch at 12:00, and supper at 5:30. Under the bridge, I ate when the opportunity presented itself.

My Institutionalized lifestyle hindered my ability to adjust to certain aspects of the vagrant lifestyle, most notably the lack of a reliable food source.

"Jesus, Emerson, slow down."

I had a whole plateful of scrambled eggs and potatoes. A whole damn Frisbee heaped hot and greasy. Hunched over, I moved without thought, driven by desire, lost in an orgy of food lust.

"Ah, leave the kid alone. He's young," Caeser was defending me, "Probably still growing. Let him eat."

"Yeah, but he's not even chewing. Man's gotta learn to enjoy his food."

Caeser chuckled, watching me. I did not care, but ate with abandon, lost in an ecstacy of satiation.

"I'd say, on that point, the kid's a natural."

I did not know hunger before. Hunger is a tyrant, a bastard, a she-devil of screaming desire. Hunger is a constant companion, an incessant chatterer of nonsense, a reaffirmation of life. Hunger is a blessing, a curse, a perverse mixture of despair and contentment. Hunger is an emotion; a lust. It certainly feels like one, anyways.

Hunger can drive a person insane.

I became Joe's accomplice, diverting attention in the produce aisle at the SuperValue up on Sixth Street, chasing an orange down the tile floor while Joe loaded his pockets with onions and fresh carrots, cans of beans, and anything else that wasn't nailed down.

"Under-ripe grapefruits' the best," he's telling me as we walked up Brewery Street to go shoplifting. I could not get used to shoplifting, not the way Joe did it. I felt armed robbery would at least maintain a person's pride. Joe scoffed at the notion of pride.

"You're not lucky enough to be proud. And I'm not dumb enough. Now, squeeze the grapefruit. Not too hard, or somebody will give you hell. Squeeze five, no more, then pick the hardest one and get it rolling down towards the bakery. Make sure there's a couple people pushing carts down there and roll it between them. Drop it, then act like a retard and kick it a few times, chasing it, and look worried until you do. Then smile, dammit Emerson, you got to learn to grin. You've got to act concerned about that damn grapefruit."

Joe's serious as hell and there I am in the SuperValue produce, kicking a damn grapefruit down the aisle like a concerned retard while he's out in canned goods, stocking up on baked beans, when a little girl reaches out and grabs the runaway fruit like it's nothing at all.

Her eyes are cool as a September breeze. She smiles and hands me the damn grapefruit.

"Hello, Mr Emerson," says her mom. Angela Blackmore, still dressed in her Heartsfield whites. So damn cool.

I grinned, swallowed hard, and that was my pride.

We had baked beans and scrambled eggs that night. They tasted good.

"Dammit, Emerson, why don't you just drink it straight out of the bottle?"

Joe was referring to the amount of ketchup I'd just applied to my beans and eggs. It's easy to forget. I'd never had to even think about ketchup before.

"Ah hell, Joe, let the kid eat. Ketchup never killed nobody." Caeser was defending me, but Joe was right; I'd used too much.

"It ain't his health I'm worried about. We've got guests, dammit. Suppose they'd like a little ketchup?"

Caeser and Franklin had to chuckle at that. Charles and Franklin were joining us for supper, and we all knew Joe didn't give a damn if they got any or not, long as he did. Leave it to Charles, though, to blow it all out of proportion.

"It's decadence, is what it is. Lot's of folks in the world would fight for a plate of beans like that. But Emerson won't eat it unless it's smothered in ketchup, even if there's hardly any left for the rest of us."

"Ah, hell. Lot's of folks don't even like ketchup, for Christ's sake." "You wanna scrape some off and smear it on yours?"

"Eat your own damn food any way you like it."

"He's trying to make it up. Dammit, give the kid a chance."

"It's too late. He's got to learn to think before he goes slopping ketchup around like there's no tomorrow."

"Dammit, Charles, you're over reacting. Nobody's ever died because of a lack of ketchup."

"The hell they ain't. Ketchup's food. Why the hell else they starving?" "Because no one gives a damn!" As soon as he said it, Caeser knew he'd

over extended. He hunched up over his plate, wishing nobody heard him. "That's my point!" Charles shouted, stabbing the air with his fork. Joe

sighed, shaking his head, but he'd started it and had nothing to bitch about. "Ketchup, nuclear waste. It's all decadence. Take what you want, forget the rest. Seventy degrees. Paradise now, to hell with tomorrow. Let Emerson have all the damn ketchup he wants."

We ate in silence then, all of us staring into the fire, avoiding eye contact. Charles was gloating, self-rightously dabbing two or three drops of ketchup sparingly about his plate, then setting the bottle down in front of Franklin.

The pot was empty and our plates scraped clean and everyone was sitting around, digesting, when Franklin picked up the bottle and began studying it, looking serious as hell as he scratched Alice's ears, her head nestled in his lap.

"You know, this ain't even ketchup. It's catsup."

Caeser guffawed triumphantly.

"That's not the point!" Charles protested.

"Ah, hell, you don't even know what you're talking about."

And off they went. Joe sighed, shaking his head and poking at the fire. Joe did not appreciate the art of arguing, he'd just as soon slip something by when you weren't looking. Franklin liked a good debate, though, and sat contentedly scratching Alice's ears, nodding his head occasionally at a point well made, regardless of who made it.

Franklin had his own way of looking at things. As he walked along, he picked facts up out of the grass and studied each without bias, confident where the path was headed.

I owed him fifteen cents. To work off my debt, I carried his sack on late night scavenger hunts. The dumpster in the alley behind Stacey's Bar yielded about ten cents worth of aluminum cans a night. Not much, but Franklin didn't need much.

Since Franklin seemed satisfied, I felt satisfied, too. It didn't matter to me, anyways. If he only made five or ten cents a night, I mean. Eventually, I came to enjoy carrying his sack, just to listen to him talk.

Franklin had theories. Quite interesting theories, some of them. For instance, he felt the earth was the center of the universe, based on the equation: (the vastness of the Universe)=pi(r2) 'r' being an unkown variable representing the distance from the earth to whatever is perceived as the universal circumference. It is a theory that is impossible to discredit, despite the fact that the earth moves through space, since 'r' is variable and no one knows how big the universe is.

"But it is impossible to prove," I argued, as Franklin crawled out of Stacey's dumpster, a paper plate glued with mustard to the sleeve of his shirt. "It's a theory, dammit," he replied, "I don't have to prove it. Either you believe it or you don't. I choose to believe it until someone proves me wrong." "Vanity," I countered,

"You create your own truths. Does it make you feel important, being the center of your universe?"

"Yes," he said, helping me pick up the last of the beer cans he'd thrown from the dumpster. He answered with conviction. We had all the cans picked up before I simply asked why.

"Because. Because I like to think it matters; that what we're doing down here matters. I like to think God has a reason to keep an eye on us. Wisdom will prevail."

I'd argued with too many counselors in my day to let that slide by. The tables had been turned too many times, and I reacted on instincts, using a vicious backhand.

"Thinking something does not make it true."

Franklin laughed and walked off down the alley, his three dogs wagging their tails and looking like happy idiots.

"That's true. But you missed the point. Wisdom will prevail. I just like to think about it. No harm in that. Hell, you can't even prove me wrong. Not beyond a reasonable doubt."

Franklin got a kick out of that, and laughed about it the rest of the night. "Be reasonable, Emerson," he kept saying.

Franklin was all right.

I thought maybe the river came down from the tundra. From way up north, where the cold meets the warmth and the sun melts the ice and the water flowed down south from there.

Franklin said the river came out of a lake, about a three week walk north. Where it came out of the lake, a person could walk across it in about six steps. He'd seen it.

I was a little disappointed when Franklin told me. I'd kind of wanted to find out for myself. I could still walk up there and have a look, but all the while I'd know what to expect.

"What the hell would you want to do that for?" Joe asked.

The three of us were sitting around after supper, digesting. The moon was full, bright over the valley, and the river was shining silver. It was surprising how bright it was, crisp and bright. It was mesmerizing. I should have never said anything about following the river around Joe, but the moon was full and I was feeling strange—all those years of not talking to anybody; there hadn't seemed to be anything worthwhile to talk about. But when I sat under a moon like that, it almost made me crazy—I could've been sitting in the rec room, smoking and watching tv, suffocating in boredom, and never even known it was out there. It made me nervous, excited, shedding a whole new light on the valley. It was wilder at night.

Caeser chuckled.

"Jesus, old man, what a question. Can't you feel it? Can't you even remember feeling it? The kid's young, for crying out loud."

Joe snorted. "Young and foolish. Sitting there with a belly full of food, and no appreciation for it. A man gets damn hungry walking up the river. And for what? Nothing but a bunch of tourists up there, wading in the water with their cameras and brochures. You'd be disappointed, son. Somebody's already done it. The river's tamed. You'd just be hungry and disappointed."

Now Caeser snorted.

"Tame, hell, that river is as wild as the day it was born. You can't tame a river like that. Not with a trillion dollars and a thousand years to try."

The two of them started arguing about the river, but I quit listening and wandered off down the valley. I climbed a ridge, found myself a rock, and sat in the moonshine, listening to the owls.

Joe was right in a way. My belly was full. But sometimes I wish I'd been born two hundred years ago. I would've followed the damn river. There wouldn't be any maps or brochures to ruin it. I could've just followed the damn river and I wouldn't have to explain it to anybody. The whole time, I'd never know how close I was or what I was going to find, until one day I'd come walking around a corner and there'd be a lake or a cave with the water running out of it and that'd be it. I wouldn't name the lake Emerson or something stupid like that. I wouldn't name it anything. I'd just camp there awhile until I felt ready, then I'd go looking for another river to follow.

Still, I had learned to appreciate the value of a full belly, despite whatever Joe thought about it. His warm and endearing personality was not the only reason I hung around the bridge that summer. By gathering firewood, hauling water, helping Joe in the SuperValue, I did everything I could to secure my next meal. Eventually, this included climbing the bridge to help Caeser with the egg harvest.

Early in the summer we enjoyed scrambled eggs four or five times a week, at Caeser's discretion. When a food source is plentiful, pigeons will keep laying to replace the stolen eggs. Caeser told me this. Caeser knew more about pigeons than anyone I've ever met. The flock's laying schedule was influenced, in part, by a harvesting system he had developed. It's called block harvesting, which meant harvesting certain sections of the bridge in rotation, therefore synchronizing the egg production of birds nesting in each section, concentrating the density of eggs and reducing the effort needed to harvest them.

I was prone to anxiety attacks at first. The steel hummed with the passing traffic, storm grates bouncing and rattling my nerves. To look down at the pigeons flying through the expanse of air beneath me, contrasting against the dark, flat river, upset my equilibrium. Sometimes the whole bridge seemed to sway and I could only hug the beam in desperation, exhausted with anxiety. "Relax, Emerson, you're making me nervous." Caeser helped me overcome my innate fear of heights by making light of the situation. At first,

I thought perhaps it was his lack of depth perception that allowed him to be so relaxed at fifty feet in the air. Eventually, I understood it was confidence.

Caeser spent hours at a time on the bridge, studying the birds. Just watching them, really. Caeser was not a man for study. No, he just liked to sit in the sunshine and feel the breeze. And talk. The man could talk for hours about pigeons.

"The thing about pigeons is that they are pure. No self-ambitions. They are part of the flock, and survive as a whole."

It was addicting. The air rose clean and fresh in the morning, rising up from the river as the sunshine broke across the water, a calm and perfect reflection of the tree covered bluffs: shades of dark green and blues. The tangy smell of the river and the warm morning sunshine got in my blood and affected my brain. I started climbing the bridge to help Caeser with the egg harvest, but eventually climbed just to climb. Following newly discovered rivers of thought, I explored Caeser's domain. Aside from an occasional sermon, he let me be.

The broods began to hatch. All around me, newborn chicks chirped for food, an impossibly weak and vulnerable sound, like a little yellow flower blooming in the cracked pavement of a twenty acre parking lot. They intrigued me. Once, I tried to hold one, a little fluff of pot-bellied yellow down. Its tiny eyes were comically defiant as it angrily pecked at my thumb. I tried to tame it, stroking its little head until it settled down and almost fell asleep. Then it lurched in panic, springing from my cupped hands and tumbling fifty feet through the air, instinctively fluttering its scrawny little wings. I never tried to hold another.

Sometimes, stretching out for my next handhold, the sight of that tumbling chick flashed through my mind. It'd be terrible; about five seconds of absolute terror. Would I scream? Would I flap my arms in a pathetic attempt at flight? Would I just drop through a haze, slipping into shock the instant I felt the loss of equilibrium and the rush of wind? At times, I could only wrap my arms around a brace and close my eyes, desperately trying to re-center myself, dazed and light headed, breathing fast and shallow, unable to move or even look down.

"The problem, Emerson, is that you expect to fall."

Caeser was almost Ludgrinian on the bridge. At times he was a shadow, a fly, a patch of rust, appearing only when noticed. It could be startling when he suddenly appeared, twenty feet away, relaxed and content in a crotch of beams, grinning because he understood.

"You're right," I answered as casually as possible, as though I'd seen him sitting there all along.

"Not necessarily", he replied, for the sake of argument. Arguing, to Caeser, was an art form, not to be taken seriously, but practiced for the sheer pleaasure of it. "If you truly expected to fall, you wouldn't be up here."

"Perhaps it's the fear of falling that brings me up here." "The fear of it, perhaps, but not the expectaton."

Sensing he'd over extended, I maneuvered for position. I hadn't won an argument all summer. Old bums can out-argue anybody. I believe that's why they're bums.

"Do you claim the ability to read my mind?"

Caeser chuckled, struck a wooden match across a patch of rust, and lit a smoke.

"I claim similar thoughts on the grounds that you and I are the only two bastards in the entire city up here. Similar thoughts, but not the same. Neither of us would admit it, even if it were true. We're proud, unlike the flock, which share the same thoughts and fly as one."

As much as I hated to admit it, I understood what he meant. I'd thought the same thing, watching the pigeons fly.

The birds were individuals, and some even became familiar to me, especially the brown and white ones. But the force of the flock ran through each, and they survived as a whole. It wasn't so obvious when they were roosting and strutting the I-beams. They were all separate then, preening themselves or feeding their chicks or just sitting there, red eyes blinking blank. But when they flew, they traveled as a unit, moving through the air as though they shared the same thoughts.

Returning from a raid on the loading docks, a swarm of birds would bank out over the river, playing the air currents, searching for an updraft, eventually circling in close to the face of the bluffs. Gaining elevation, as though climbing a spiral staircase, flapping their wings and working hard, they rose till they were above the height of the bridgedeck, about sixty yards out. Then in unison, they shortened their wings strokes, descending into a low, sweeping arc, gaining speed and momentum, gliding lower and lower, faster and faster, until smoothly, they'd sweep up through the air and come shooting through the steel webbing like feathered rockets. Just as they cleared the webbing, they spread their wings with a 'pop,' leaned back, and landed on the I-beams soft as a short hop.

Climbing the bridge evolved into something of a passion for me. It was a source of pride. I felt a degree of satisfaction in overcoming my fear. As the summer wore on, facing my fear became almost routine.

Foolish pride. The expectation of fear diminishes its impact. I didn't understand that yet.

The summer turned hot, slow and lazy. With the appearance of the broods, the egg harvest was officially over. The birds were left to raise the chicks, renewing the strength of the flock. Joe and Caeser slept through most of the day, stretched out in the cool shade beneath the bridge. Franklin and his dogs grew lethargic in the heat, even Alice barely acknowledging me with a few short flips of her tail when I stopped in for a visit. The days were long, and grew heavy with boredom. Boredom can drive a person insane. Out of desperation, I'd go see Charles.

Charles lived in an abandoned boxcar, a rusted Canadian Pacific. It sat at the base of the bluff, stripped of its undercarriage and left behind when the tracks were torn up and the railyard moved south to the present day loading docks. The boxcar was hidden in a tangle of brush and trees, cottonwoods and aspen that had seeded down from the ravines and ridges of the riverbank. To see it, faded into a forgotten corner of the valley, stranded in the thick trees, stirs the imagination.

Like it'd been deposited there by a great, powerful flood instead of the slow, creeping waters of time. I'm sure that boxcar is still down there, and I'd like to go see it again someday.

It was green, when it was new. It's mostly rusted now, but the pitted steel carries patches of heavy green paint here and there. A suggestion of white lettering arched across its side panels: The Canadian Pacific Railroad.

It was a good home, dry and secure. Aside from the skunks which burrowed beneath it to litter and hibernate, Charles was well served. After five years, Charles no longer attempted to dislodged the skunks, and a truce had been achieved. Occasionally, a young excitable skunk or an anxious mother skunk would let him have it when Charles stumbled out to relieve himself in the dead of night. But his habit of muttering usually provided plenty of warning, and encounters had become rare.

The same with visitors. Although he was a friendly enough host, Charles did not get much company. The skunks discouraged guests, but it was mostly Charles' madness which caused his isolation. Or perhaps it was his isolation that caused his madness. There had come a point, years before I met him, when it no longer mattered. Charles was an alloy of madness and isolation, of anger and loneliness. He was a victim of his own principles, based on truths most men refuse to acknowledge; which forced him to continuously reaffirm those truths. This was his madness. He knew it, and it angered him. Only through his discipline was he able to keep it from erupting in a fury to self-destruction. The anger smoldered and sometimes boiled dangerously in his veins when fueled by yet another reaffirmation of the hateful truth.

Ceaser thought Charles crazy, and dismissed him as mad. Yet there were positive aspects of Charles madness that Caeser refused to appreciate. Caeser spent his summer nights sleeping under the bridge and his winters in constant search for warmth; a man with a robust lust for comfort and physical pleasure, but who enjoyed them only when achieved without sacrifice. Charles paid dearly and Caeser dismissed him as mad but, despite the skunks, Charles slept comfortably in his boxcar, ate at a table, and read books at night in the glow of an oil lamp. When it rained, he was dry and when it snowed, he lit a fire in the woodstove, drank coffee, and listened to music on a battery powered radio.

The boxcar was insulated with blue styrofoam pilfered from a local construction site and glued to the walls. Several throw rugs were stretched out on the floor and a large, wooden spool was turned on end and served as a table, over which a clean cloth was draped, along with a vase of some sort of dried weeds or maybe even fresh flowers. Charles showered regularly at the YMCA and swept the boxcar out damn near every day. Five wooden shelves, salvaged from and old pallet, were lined with books: Steinbeck, Ferber, Faulkner. Charles held a job washing towels and jock straps at the YMCA, some sort of program for crazy vets. This steady income enabled him to purchase his food, unlike Joe, and he had a well stocked pantry of canned vegetables. His clothes, although not new, were certainly not cast-offs, and he visited a regular barber every couple months. He was a proud man, applying liberal amounts of

Old Spice to compete with the low odor of skunk. Sometimes, when the breeze was right, you could smell Charles half a minute before you saw or heard him coming dowm the path.

Sometimes we'd go fishing. Charles went fishing every Wednesday. It was his day off, and he spent it down by the power plant with a can of worms and a spool of line. It was a four mile walk along the river down to the power plant, a nice walk along the exposed gravel and sand bars below the steep riverbanks. Sometimes we'd find old, skinny tires off Model T's or pieces of furniture, tables and chairs, or even coiled pieces of copper tubing from an old moonshiner's still. But since Charles was going fishing, he never wanted to stop and look around, ignoring whatever might be washed up on shore, no matter how interesting.

"Charles, you've got to learn to cherish the moment."

"It's too damn distracting. Ludgrin was a fool. A spectator, focusing on every damn moment that came along."

"He won a Pulitzer," I said, compelled to defend Ed's honor for the sake of argument.

"There isn't any rule that says fools can't win Pulitzers. A man's got to learn to focus on what matters."

Charles was the most single minded person I've ever met.

The power plant lay in a wide, flat expanse of the valley, where the bluffs spread out wide and the river divides into several channels. With its reactors and cooling towers, the plant looked strangely out of place on the flats. The river meandered slow and easy, shallow and warm through the low islands of tall coarse grass and stunted willow trees. The pools of warm, stagnant water provided ideal carp habitat, and with the power plant humming it the dense, humid air, we waded the back channels. Setting out baited hooks on the muddy bottom, unwinding the spools, we slowly backed up to shore, careful not to spook the fish sneaking around our feet. There we'd sit, the sunshine warm and the air thick, dragonflies darting over the water, listening to the red-winged blackbirds singing from the tops of cattails, the electric sound of cicadas buzzing through sharp and crisp. At least, I was listening. Charles waited for a fish. He thought a three pound carp was damn exciting.

"Set the hook!" he would suddenly yell, as though I were in the path of a speeding truck. Across the mirrored surface of the water, my line's headed out deep and in a flash of panic I would inevitably jerk the bait free of the fish, despite its best effort to hang onto it. Setting a hook properly requires technique. My lack of techinque disgusted Charles. He had no patience. His lack of patience disgusted me. We soon grew irritated with each other, and Wednesday mornings I climbed the bridge to avoid going fishing with him and watched him sneak through the willows below camp, with a can of worms, doing his best to avoid me.

The SuperValue up on Sixth Street went out of business that summer.

I guess it couldn't compete with the big stores opening up out in the suburbs. Charles associated it with nuclear waste. He claimed it was just another example of corporate greed monopolizing the market. He began a crusade. He wrote a letter to the editor protesting against the emasculation of the neighborhood.

Joe and Charles formed something of an alliance over the store closing. Joe missed the hell out of the SuperValue. We all did. The stew thinned out considerably. Joe took to self-rightously cursing the greedy, short-sighted corporate elitists right along with Charles, bumming cigarettes and egging him on. We were all kind of enthused about the letter. Except Caeser, who ridiculed the whole thing. Every night Charles would come over and read his letter to us, and Joe and I would make suggestions. Joe's the one who came up with the 'emasculation of the neighborhood' phrase. "The Emasculation Proclamation." Caeser called it. It was a let down when it failed to get published. Charles took it hardest.

"Lookit this," he'd shake the paper at us. "Baseball. Six pages devoted to nothing but baseball!"

"Dammit, Charles, lots of people like baseball," Caeser'd argue, "What the hell do you expect?"

Caeser was right—Charles knew better. But Charles was a martyre, and martyres are irritating.

They idealize suffering. Martyres go hungry even if they don't have to. Bums avoid suffering. Bums view suffering as a consequence of a miscalculation. Although they often share the same space, the motives of bums and martyres are broadly divergent. A martyre protests the greed, while a bum tries to get around it with as little effort as posible.

Charles wrote a letter to the editor protesting the store closing and the unfairness of corporate greed. Caeser taught me how to snare pigeons and survive.

There isn't much to a pigeon. The meat is dark and tough, but if properly stewed and seasoned it makes a good broth. I did not enjoy snaring pigeons, but Caeser convinced me it was part of managing the great flock of birds.

"The thing about pigeons is that they are pure," he explained, showing me how to set a fishline snare. "They trust routine. A routine is the wisdom of the flock, learned over generations."

Taking advantage of this trust, we set the snares across commonly used flight paths in the lower webbing of the bridge; places where the pigeons shot through hard and fast, popping their wings to lose momentum. Caeser knew the location of the paths, and using three foot lengths of fishline, secured one end to a nearby rivet hole, positioning the snare in place with a bit of chewing gum. The gum held the snare ready, and allowed it to snap freely. If the birds didn't spread their wings to lose momentum, they would've shot right through. But their spread wings caught the snare, and it snapped tight around their necks. Most of the time the birds were traveling at such a high rate of speed and the fishline cut so sharp they were instantly decapitated, their bodies fluttering down into the willows or out over the railroad tracks without the rest of the flock aware of what was happening. Sometimes, though, a bird just hung there, struggling against the snare, and needed to be bounced. It had to be done quickly, as a snagged and fluttering bird alerts the flock, and the flight paths shift. I hated bouncing birds, and the whole concept of snaring did not appeal to me. But as Caeser said, it was part of managing the great flock of pigeons.

"Do not be afraid to draw strength from the flock, Emerson. For you, too, must survive."

I wasn't afraid of snaring pigeons. I just didn't care for it much.

Charles continued to harass me about the goatskull picture.

It was insulting as hell. Charles was acting as though it were my fault. The fact that the Mayor was so damn concerned about my teeth, that is. Charles was mad.

"Hell, it ain't the kid's fault." Caeser was sitting in his chair and enjoying a cigarette. I resented him calling me a kid, but I didn't say anything. I was sulking. Sulking is different from apathy. You've got to care to sulk. It's half a step above apathy. I did not enjoy sulking, but Charles was being unreasonable. He wanted me to write a letter to the editor, denouncing the mayor for worrying about my teeth instead of trying to avert a nuclear disaster. I refused, because Charles was implying that I was somehow responsible for the mayor's cavity crusade. It irritated the hell out of me. Besides, my flea problem had returned. It was disconcerting. Although the population was still relatively low, I now understood the ramifications of a full blown flea infestation, and shuddered at the thought. Nuclear poisoning paled in comparison. I'd never been poisoned before.

"That's right," Charles was excited. He kept waving the stupid picture around, his eyes huge in his glasses. "It's not his fault and it's not your fault. Hell, it isn't even the mayor's fault. We're all victims. All just innocent victims. A whole damn nation of victims."

Joe sighed, examining his toes through a hole in his sock, spreading them apart as though expecting to find something.

Charles thought I was posing for the stupid picture, my hands folded humbly before me. He often assumed the pose when he was trying to irritate me, squinting and trying to look tough.

"Just what the hell do you expect him to do, for crying out loud?" Caeser was defending me because it put him at odds with Charles. Caeser was foolish to argue with him, but he could not stand to let Charles have the last word. Caeser was crazier than Charles, but in a different way. Caeser looked crazy with his wild hair and beard and eye patch, his one eye shining bright and reckless through the whole tangled mess. Charles looked like he might work in a library or something. Except when he got excited.

"Nothing!" Charles shouted, getting to his feet. "Absolutely nothing. Everybody is expected to do nothing. Let them store their damn nuclear waste anywhere they want."

Charles was walking away up the red rock path, shouting like a madman. "Not a God damn thing!"

Joe sighed, putting his shoe back on.

Caeser chuckled and dug out another cigarette, crumpled the empty pack and tossed it into the fire.

"Talks damn smart for a man living in a skunk infested boxcar. That's the problem with Charles. He don't think reality. Just because he has a point don't mean the world's going to stop and listen to him. And the dumb son of a bitch is mad 'cause they won't. You know what Charles needs?"

Caeser paused, waiting for me to answer. He knew Joe wouldn't. Joe was acting half asleep, staring at the fire.

"What?" I said, even though I was sulking. I was getting tired of sulking, anyways. There's not much point in sulking if no one seems to notice.

"A woman. Charles needs a woman to argue with. It's a basic need of his to argue. Why else does he come down here? To talk about the weather? Sports? Fishing? All he ever does is argue with us."

He should have said me, not us. Caeser and Charles argued if they got within twenty feet of each other.

"The thing is, she'd have to be crazy. And stubborn. And tough." Joe cocked one eye up at Caeser.

"If you're talking about Rose, you're crazier than Charles." Caeser smiled and just stood there, looking up at the smoke. "Let me think on it. I'm getting an idea."

Joe sighed and looked back at the fire, his eyelids drooping low.

The next morning, Caeser was nudging me with his boot and telling me to get up.

"Let's go, Emerson. Cupid appeared to me in a dream last night and has shown me a way."

I had no idea what he was talking about, but I rolled out anyways. As much as I hated to admit it, my survival depended to a large extent on Caeser and Joe. I usually got up when they told me to.

Joe was crouched beside the fire, maneuvering the

coffee pot around to keep it boiling without scorching. Joe was good about things like that. He was in a bad mood, though. Scowling and rubbing his chest. He was infested. He wasn't blaming me directly, though more than likely I'd been the vehicle of transmission. I was not allowed to sit in Joe's chair because of my flea condition, and I did whenever he wasn't around. But it was Franklin whom he held most responsible—Franklin and his dogs.

"Man living with dogs," he snorted. "It ain't healthy. Crawling with fleas and scratching like a dog."

A flea bit me on the stomach. Casually, I rubbed myself, trying to cripple the bastard without appearing too obvious.

"You get used to them after awhile," I said halfheartedly. Fleas really are miserable. I was getting used to them, but they still drove me crazy sometimes. Embarrassing as hell, too.

"Hell, that ain't the point," Joe jerked and twisted an arm up behind his back. "A man can get used to anything, if that's his philosophy. Man's gotta draw his lines somewhere and stick to them. I don't want to get used to them, dammit. I've got my principles. Man with fleas ain't no better than a dog."

There was no arguing with Joe when he started talking about his principles, so I let it drop.

It was a nice, cool morning and I wanted to sit around and drink coffee. A pair of geese came flying low up the river, calling to each other, their voices echoing crisp and loud. In unison, they glided lower and lower to the water, touching down in a long, gliding 'v' that radiated out behind them. They floated side by side, occasionally calling out as though laughing at a joke between them.

"Romance!" Caeser said. "That's the order of the day. We must save our friend Charles from the madness of his loneliness. We must find him a woman he can treasure and argue with for the rest of his life. I've got a plan."

Joe sighed.

"Look, Caeser. Rose doesn't even like you. How do you figure you're going to talk her into Charles, who doesn't like you, either?"

"Love will overcome all obstacles. The details will work themselves out. The point is, I'm doing something, and even Charles himself would have to admit the merits of my actions. Let's go, Emerson."

I didn't say anything, but simply followed Caeser up the park path. It was steep and dangerous, worn deep into the riverbank by feet long since moved on. Exposed tree roots reached out to trip you, and it was a thirty foot drop from the top. Caeser knew the path well, but I had to use caution.

"Let's go, Emerson. Cupid's work must not be delayed."

The brewery third shift workers get off work at seven in the morning and walk across the parking lot to buy Rose's coffee and a bismark in the little park where the Indian battle took place. The coffee is hot and strong and Rose knows most of the guys by name, but she doesn't say much unless she's giving odds on baseball games. Rose knows more about baseball than anybody alive, and she'll bet on it.

The thirdshifters were standing around in little bunches, drinking coffee from styrofoam cups and talking smart. The guys are always standing around with their hardhats and lunch boxes, and it's a good thing because there's pigeon shit all over the park benches.

Rose's brown hair was turning grey, and she looked bored and tough, but she was damn pretty. Especially when she smiled, which wasn't often. In a way, Rose was phony, because she was always acting so tough and bored. But it was attractive on Rose. It was her make-up. If she would've acted happy and perky all the time, she would've looked stupid. Apathy looked good on Rose.

It'd been hard for me to get to know Rose because she wouldn't talk to me at first. She never said much anyways. It's easier to be tough when you don't talk; as though she didn't give a damn about any of it. But sometimes when she's cleaning up and no one's around, she talks about things, just to talk, but it wasn't politics or even baseball, but real things—like she's going to wallpaper her apartment or change the water-pump in the station wagon on Sunday or her sister who's married and has kids and lives out in Plymouth with a yard and a cat. She says her nephews are the best kids in the world and make her cards on her birthday. You could tell Rose got a kick out of those cards. I bet she taped them to her refridgerator. Rose was kind of phony, in a way.

She didn't like bums. Rose held a biased opinion of bums. That was because of Caeser. Rose didn't like Caeser. I think she did, though, more than she let on, anyways.

Caeser sold some of the pigeon eggs to the guys who worked the third-shift at the brewery. He'd conned some of them into thinking pigeon eggs were some kind of aphrodisiac, giving a guy a sustained hard-on. He swore his eye had been scratched out by a prostitute in Alabama, though he was probably lying. Claimed women went insane lying beneath him, and it was all on account of a steady diet of pigeon eggs. "Make sure she clips her fingernails first," was the solemn advice he passed along with each sale. Of course, the guys buying the eggs always exaggerated the results when bragging about their exploits, and demand grew. Six for a buck was the going rate when Caeser made them available. The eggs were in such demand that sometimes guys would fight over who got to purchase them. Rose thought Caeser was a trouble making con-man. He was, basically.

We'd just gotten into the park when this big guy comes pushing out of the crowd and bellering at Caeser like a bull.

"If it ain't the one-eyed pirate himself. Up before noon and up to no good, I would imagine. You got any of those eggs with you?"

Murphy was one of Caeser's best customers. Murphy was all right. Just loud as hell, with a big red face and a big belly that stuck out tight against his t-shirt. The New York Giants had given him a try-out for offensive guard in the seventies, but he'd been cut because of a bum knee. Murphy was harmless. Just loud as hell. He talked loud and belched loud, laughed loud and farted loud, often at the same time. He thought Caeser was the funniest son of a bitch who ever lived.

"It's your lucky day, Murph." Caeser was talking almost as loud as Murphy. A lot of the guys are looking over at us, and I feel embarrassed in my corduroy sports suit next to a wild man selling pigeon eggs. Some of them aren't looking too friendly, either. No one says anything, though. Caeser's long arms and those big hands dangling loose and his wild eye and scruffy beard— he looked like the kind of guy who'd bite off your ear and swallow it whole. Caeser's got half a dozen eggs in a little brown bottle sack, and Murphy digs out a dollar and damn near runs off with the bag. He slaps his arm around Caeser and drags him up to Rose's stationwagon where she's got her coffee maker set up on the tailgate with two boxes of rolls. One's marked 'Day Old' and the other's marked 'Fresh', and Rose is busy shooing off flies and taking a bet on the night's game between Minnesota and Cleveland. "Minnesota, I get one and pay one-fifty per."

The guy doesn't want to give, but Rose doesn't budge and he finally gives in a bet for five dollars and buys a sweetroll, and Rose drops the money into her apron.

"Rose," Murphy bellows, "Let's set these guys up with a cup and a roll.

Sweetroll, that is."

And Murphy laughs at his joke, but Rose doesn't even smile.

"Hello, Rose." Caeser says with a note of humility that catches me off guard. Caeser is rubbing his beard as though trying to groom himself and acting sincere as hell as he accepts the cup of coffee and a longjohn out of the day old box. Phony as hell. I'm thinking he's over reaching because whatever it is he's trying to pull, Rose is on to him. Rose is sharp, and she'll know something is up.

Rose goes on polishing her coffee maker, and Murphy's showing the guys his pigeon eggs like a big kid with a bag of candy he's not going to share. Caeser's standing there politely drinking his coffee, and I just hung around waiting to see what he's trying to pull.

"Rose, I got five for Oakland at one-fifty," Caeser says, trying to sound casual.

Rose waited a second, and then kind of snorted. "The hell you do."

Caeser moved in.

"You're right. You're God damn right, Rose. You know me, and you know I'm a bullshitter and a thief. It's what I been and it's what I'll be. But right now, for just this one moment, I'm going to tell it like I see it. I like you Rose. You're all right. And I'm crazy enough to tell you I've found your perfect match. Charles ain't no bum, just mad as hell. Smarter than hell, in his own way. Damn smart. Too smart for his own good, you know what I mean. He could be entertaining as hell to the right woman. That's it, Rose. Anything after this could be pure bullshit. I'm not promising anything."

Rose just stood there, rhythmically polishing her coffee maker, glancing at Caeser like he was crazy and acting bored. It was an attractive emotional state on Rose. It epitomized her. She rubbed the coffee maker like she didn't give a damn about nothing.

"Caeser, you're so weird," she finally said, signaling the end of the conversation.

Caeser threw back his head and laughed. "I know, sister, I know."

And Murphy's giggling like a kid with his bag of pigeon eggs, and me and Caeser each got another cup of coffee and a bismark out of the fresh box. Even Rose smiled when he tipped her a buck.

After a couple weeks of thin stew, our luck finally took a turn for the better. To our amazement, a farmer's market began to be held every Saturday morning in the brewery parking lot. It was organized by the bed and breakfast establishments to promote the brewery district and to procure fresh produce for their clientele. It went over well, attracting as many as fifty vendors and hundreds of health conscious consumers on any given Saturday morning. A crowded and chaotic affair, it restored Joe's faith in the system. His stew improved dramatically. Our spirits lifted. The farmer's market brought prosperity to the valley.

The mayor even showed up a couple times, dressed down in a casual sweater and jeans, carrying a basket of tomatoes and cucumbers, shaking hands with the folks, looking relaxed and informal. Except for his hair. You could spot the mayor's head halfway across the parking lot. It gave him a sense of poise, even when dressed in a goofy looking sweater you could tell his wife probably knitted for him as a project in some night class. Mrs Mckinnley was a nice looking woman. She looked like a mother, I mean. Not fat, just kind of plump and serious looking as she picked over a pile of tomatoes, loading the basket her husband carried on his elbow. She was there to buy vegetables, and while her husband hammed it up for the cameras, she was busy thumping muskmelons, even smelling them, right in front of everybody, like she didn't care if her husband got elected or not, as long as she got a good melon.

With their dark suits and shades, the mayor's bodyguards were always shadowing him just out of camera range. I recognized the one who was afraid of dragonflies and nodded at him, thinking we had something in common. He ignored me, or at least didn't acknowledge me. With his dark glasses, he was hard to read, but I got the impression he was watching me, and didn't like what he saw. Joe and I usually gave the mayor a wide berth at the Market. The crowded market provided Joe with a perfect working environment.

I simply carried a basket and meandered through the crowd, artificial distractions being unnecessary, ignoring Joe when he brushed by, slipping in a cucumber or an ear of corn as he passed. Aside from having to carry the basket while Joe shopped, I enjoyed Saturday mornings, mingling with the crowd and pretending to be just a normal shopper. There was always plenty to see. Magicians and jugglers put on remarkable little shows for spare dollar bills. Sometimes I'd drop a tomato in their hat out of appreciation. Joe would get mad if he caught me, but it made me feel better, and I'd do it anyways. Once, a para-sailor sponsored by the big mall out in Bloomington attempted to jump off the brewery and soar over the crowd. Apparently he was planning to catch an updraft off the bluffs, but the air current failed and instead he sailed down into the parking lot, slamming into a pile of cabbage. The guy broke an arm and Joe tried making sauerkraut, but it smelled so bad no one would eat it.

I enjoyed Saturday mornings for a change of pace. It was just nice to be around regular people once and awhile.

"Such a Mess. Greed is Rampant. Decadence is Rampant."

"Every man has within his character the strain of genius that would enable humanity to blossom. Every man has within his character the strain of genius that would reduce humanity to a rotting corpse. It is the ability to choose which produces the struggle, first within a man's soul, then within the society in which he was born."

Caeser paused to reflect on his words, drawing inspiration from the pint being passed around the fire. Franklin nodded his head in somber agreement, stroking the head of the black dog nestled in his lap. Joe looked like he might be asleep, chin down on his chest, except he never let the bottle slip by without servicing. It was the third bottle. Joe had lifted three pints of Canadian wisky from somewhere up in the brewery district. Charles had brought beer. I was having an out-of-body experience, rushes which carried me up with the smoke and sparks dancing off the red glow of the fire. It felt almost sacred, the buzz of the alcohol and Caeser's eloquence, as though we were on the cusp of a distant horizon, about to witness vistas of knowledge never before seen by man. It was humbling. I was humbled. I did not speak, but simply floated above the men, my thoughts rising with the sparks till they cooled and disappeared into the night. Jesus, was I drunk.

Charles was poking at the fire, stirring up the sparks and looking irritated.

Caeser was irritating him.

"But what the hell has that got to do with nuclear waste?"

Caeser nodded the bottle at him, and Joe reached out and took it. "Chemicals," Caeser said. "It's all chemicals. Yet our thoughts are not chemicals. They are the breath of a man's soul, rising from a vat of cerebral juices. The chemicals mix and simmer, and within a man's soul a burning desire grows and the chemicals start to boil. Some fires flicker and soon die, producing little waste, which is soon broken down by stomach acids and end up in the sewer plant. Others grow in intensity. It starts a chain reaction, like nuclear fission, that carries itself along, growing stronger, the soul burning white hot, till the heat of the reaction becomes too much. A man burns out, melts down, and what is left? A pool of poison chemicals. Nobody wants anything to do with nuclear waste."

Franklin nodded his head in agreement. Joe was snoring lightly and scratching himself. Charles just shook his head and got up to leave, rustling his newspaper back in order.

"That has got absolutely nothing to do with storing nuclear waste on the greatest watershed in the nation."

Franklin nodded his head in agreement. Caeser emptied the bottle and tossed it at the red embers, scattering sparks.

"Perhaps not," Caeser said. "But look, Charles. It's a percentage thing. You try to beat the System, you're gonna lose. You let them build their nuclear dump, there's a good chance you never suffer the consequences."

Charles shook his head again. The flames reflecting on his glasses had an eerie effect, as though Charles were burning up inside.

"No. No, dammit, that's not right. We are not simply spectators. Moments can be produced. There comes a time when a person must interact to produce a moment. It is the consequences of my inaction for which I hold the greater fear."

Ed Ludgrin had been there. It was unmistakable. His madness had somehow melded with Charles' version, creating a sort of hybrid of momentcular insanity.

Before Caeser could reply, Charles stepped out of the firelight, disappearing around the red rock and rustling up the darkness of the path. Franklin's dogs wimpered, their ears alert as they listened to him leave.

"Guess it's time for me to go, too." Franklin said, and his three dogs stood up expectantly at the sound of aluminum cans rattling. There was something of interest to the dogs in the sack. They probed it with their noses as Franklin stood there.

"Raccoon," he said, "up on Seventh Street. Dogs caught it coming out of the storm sewer. Fat rascal. Lots of fat this year, and it's still early. Could be a brutal winter coming. Twice as much fat as last year."

Me and Caeser simply nodded. Neither of us wanted to see the raccoon in death. You know it'd look cynical.

Franklin walked off down the blue rock path, his dogs chasing ahead of him and yelping in the brush. A big diesel truck, a brewery truck, came roaring down the hill on the far side of the valley, downshifting low and tearing apart the night. The iron storm grates jumped and rattled as the truck passed overhead. Caeser went off to roll up and Joe was just sitting there, chin on his chest. I'd let him be, but he's drunk and might roll forward and land in the fire.

"Joe," I said, "roll up. It's late."

"Fuck you," Joe replied, still sitting there when I rolled up behind the red rock. It was a cool night, and I was glad for my two blankets. They were heavy and warm. I just laid under the blankets, listening to the traffic and the crickets were chirping. Lots of crickets. Thousands, I bet. Crickets are bastards in a way. They climb between the blankets and hide in my shoes. They're smooth and slick and squirmy. Not as bad as fleas, though.

After a few minutes I heard Joe drag himself up with a sigh and go stumbling down into the willows, where he rolled up in the shadows.

In the grey of the morning there's a truck coming across the bridge with its engine revving and air-brakes rapping, but the echoes roll soft and muffled in the thick air. My mind's thick and I don't want to get up. Joe's making coffee and he's told me to get up twice already, but it feels like I'm under six feet of water and can't move.

"C'mon, Emerson. We gotta get up there before it rains. Damn, it's going to be a cold rain. Nothing will ruin the market like a cold rain."

It was Saturday morning. I usually look forward to the farmer's market, but this morning I'm feeling thick and slow.

A wave of pigeons were returning from a raid on the loading docks, a swarm of greys. There's a brown and white one on the edge, and even in the dim light it looks fresh and new. The birds arc low and then shoot up through the bracing, but I can't hear their wings popping; the air's so thick it smothers the sound.

I don't feel like going anywhere. The air is heavy and there's a feeling down through the valley, heavy and dull, so that I'd rather just lay under the blankets, but Joe keeps telling me to get up. He's anxious to get going, and he's in a bad mood because of the fleas.

"Man, how can you just lay there, crawling with the bastards? I can't stand it. They're driving me nuts. God damn dogs," he says, trying to reach a spot up between his shoulder blades, can't, and begins rubbing against the blue rock, disgust on his face. "I gotta do something about it. I can't go through the winter like this. I'm telling you, Emerson, they're making me crazy. Can't concentrate with the bastards sneaking around on me. Emerson, get up or I'm tossing out your coffee."

He would've, too. Joe was in a bad mood. Fleas really are miserable. But it was the weather affecting Joe's attitude as much as the fleas. Pushing down from the north, already the breeze was getting stronger. The willows bent and swayed, yellow cottonwood leaves starting to spin down from the banks overhead. It smelled like rain, a tangy, spicy smell, and Joe was right, it was going to be a cold one.

Caeser was still rolled up next to the footing. The breeze swirled through and he's all hunched and curled up, and he's freezing. He's only got one blanket left after selling me his other two back when the nights were getting warmer and autumn seemed like a long way off. Joe's smoking a cigarette and drinking his coffee, but I'm clean out of smokes. The augers were grinding low and another bunch of pigeons came swarming up from the docks, all grey. I'd just like to sit awhile and try to clear my head. Everything's thick and muffled, but Joe's in a hurry to get to the market before the rain, and he's finished his cigarette.

We stopped to catch our breath at the top of the bank. The thirdshifters were in Brewery Park, buying coffee and sweetrolls. Rose's stationwagon was there and she's wearing her apron, handing out styrofoam cups of steaming coffee. Joe saw I was going to stop and talk to Rose, so he resigned himself and stood off to the side, looking half asleep.

"How's it going today, Emerson?" she says, and sets me up a cup filled almost to the rim, winking to let me know it's free and right away I know something is up. Rose is smart and doesn't survive by giving free coffee to bums.

"Minnesota is in the series," she said with a shrug when she saw me thinking about it. Then she tried to look bored, polishing her coffee maker.

"That's great," I said.

Rose quit polishing and looked at me.

"Look, if you don't want it, I can dump it back in." She held out her hand for the cup.

"No. No, I mean it. That's great."

I took a sip. It was a cool morning and the coffee tasted good. Rose was all right. She started polishing again.

"You bums drive me crazy. How come you want to be a bum, Emerson?

You like them guys?"

She raised her chin over at Joe, who was standing off by himself looking out across the parking lot, ignoring everything and missing nothing: all wrinkled up and sunken in and dirty looking.

"Yeah, I guess so."

Rose served up a couple of fresh bismarks and a round of coffee for one of the third shift groups. The guys were talking about the game and kidding Rose that she was dating Cleveland's pitcher and wearing him out before the big games. Rose made a disparaging remark concerning the guy's ability to make love to a woman, and they got a charge out of that and started making lewd jokes amongst themselves. Rose shoved them off and went back to her polishing.

"I guess so," I repeated, "But they're not my idols, if that's what you mean."

Rose laughed. Rose was damn pretty when she smiled.

"You'd have to be crazy. How come, then? I mean, I can see Caeser doing it because he likes it. And Joe, he's sneakier than a hungry cat. They're bums. But you don't like it. That's plain. Maybe you're trying to learn to like it, but I don't see why."

I just kind of shrugged. Rose looked at me from a detached viewpoint. "It's stupid. Just wasting your luck on a bunch of nickel games is all I can

see. Caeser pawning off pigeon eggs for two dollars a dozen. Playing the clown and daring someone to laugh. Lying and bragging and talking nonsense. You've heard him. Telling me about some guy named Charles, when I really give a shit, you know?"

That was it. That explained the free coffee, I mean. Rose was working me. I couldn't help but feel some disappointment in her. Joe was right—neither Charles nor Rose liked Caeser. In a way, they were both phony. It was all they had in common though. Rose was smart, Charles was crazy. And Caeser walks up and belches out a prophecy, and just like that Rose is thinking there might be something to it. What really got me, though, was that she should've known better. Maybe Caeser was right—love overcomes all obstacles. Maybe it blurred Rose's common sense of Caeser being nothing but a bullshitter and a thief. It's what he's been, and it's what he'll be. Don't give me any of this 'except for this one moment' crap.

Rose was polishing her coffee maker like she doesn't give a damn about any of it, and I was trying to think of something to say when Joe comes over and says it's time to go.

"It's going to rain, Emerson. We gotta go."

Then Murphy sees me talking to Rose and hails, pushing through the crowd belly first, spilling coffee. Joe sighed and Murphy's laughing as he came.

"Where the hell is that one-eyed pirate?"

Murphy enjoyed the hell out of himself, and he thought Caeser was the funniest son of a bitch who ever lived. I told him Caeser was still sleeping, and Murphy started bellering about that.

"Damn, you guys have got it made. No alarm clocks, no time clocks.

Time don't mean nothing to you guys, does it?"

Joe sighed again. Murphy was all right, just kind of loud.

"Say, you got any of them eggs with you?" Murphy bought the eggs with gusto, and you know he chased his wife, Ruth, around the room after making a big deal out of eating them. I was going to tell him about the pigeons being done laying for the year, but he wouldn't shut up.

"I'll tell you guys what," he says, pulling out his wallet. "I'll give you four bucks for a dozen of them eggs. I'll give you two today, and two more when you bring them. How's that sound?"

I started telling him about the pigeons being done laying but before I can say anything, Joe's got the two dollars in his coat pocket—hardly even saw his hands move. Murphy barely had the money clear of his wallet and there's a blur and kind of a suckering sound, and Joe's walking off across the parking lot, Murphy just standing there with his wallet out, looking uncertain about everything. I didn't say anything about the pigeons then. He didn't want to hear it, and I didn't want to cause trouble. I just shrugged and told Murphy I'd see about them eggs. Rose snorted, shook her head, and lit herself a cigarette, polishing her coffee maker like she didn't give a damn about any of it. Apathy looked good on Rose.

I started after Joe, but he wasn't waiting and I refused to run to catch up. It made me mad the way he'd lifted Murphy's two dollars when he knew damn well there wasn't going to be any eggs until next spring. Murphy was all right. Kind of loud, but there wasn't any point in hurting his feelings.

The traffic was heavy at the First Street intersection, a line of cars backed up and idling on the bridge. The cars were full of judgement and I tried to avoid eye contact, forcing myself not to chase fleas. I was feeling moody. My suit was filthy and my hair was long and wild and I felt like a bum. I just shuffled along with the basket, eyes down in the gutter—dried cottenwood leaves and dirty bits of styrofoam and cigarette butts and plastic wrappers. And a dead pigeon.

A brown and white pigeon, hollow eyed and cynical. I nudged it with my foot, but it was stiff and cold. There were always a few dead pigeons laying around. Pigeons are nearsighted and keep hitting powerlines or smacking into windows, but this was the first dead brown and white pigeon I'd ever seen. There were about twenty other pigeons up on the brewery, strutting along the cornice, but they were all anonymous greys. The brown and white ones were sort of special to me. They always looked brand new.

Although irritated with him, I wanted to talk to Joe about it. I just wanted to know if he'd seen it, too. Joe knew the flock pretty well. He'd appreciate the novelty of a dead brown and white pigeon, and not think it strange that I should mention it. Bums have a unique sense of intrigue.

He was standing with a bunch of thirdshifters, hardhats and lunch boxes, waiting for the lights to change. I started to hurry, dodging through the sidewalk traffic. The light changed, people began moving and I wasn't paying attention. Just as I was about to catch up to Joe, this guy stepped out in front of me and I ran right into him.

He was a big, serious looking guy in a dark suit and shaded glasses. He kind of grabbed me in surprise, me ramming into him like that. It was the mayor's bodyguard, the one who's afraid of dragonflies. He scowled. Instinctively, I scowled back.

We scowled at one another, though he clearly had the edge, being well fed and healthy. He had hold of my arm, and his grip tightened. Then I thought of something. Changing my facial expression to that of horror and disbelief, I stared at the spot where his broad shoulders met his thick neck.

"What in the hell is that?" I said. It worked, just for an instant. He backed up, loosening his grip, just for a second, until he realized he'd been tricked, but I was already slipping past him. He tried to grab me again and I jerked free and he stepped forward and I pushed him back and as I tried to spin away and get lost in the crowd, I ran right into the mayor, who grabbed my hand and started shaking it.

There were three or four tv cameras and half a dozen reporters and the red lights were flickering right at me. The mayor didn't recognize me. I'd lost weight since he'd talked to me and Franklin earlier in the summer. My hair was long and my face was dirty with a lean growth of whiskers, but he knew who I was. A miserable misfit. He asked for my name and how long it'd been since I'd seen a dentist.

"Fourteen years! Fourteen years Mr Smith has had to face life without proper dental care. Or Republican care, for that matter. For they do not care what happens to the unfortunate souls, those souls displaced by the system of greed designed to accumulate wealth to an elitist class. Their fingernails are manicured, while Mr Smith's teeth rot in his head."

He started talking about festering wounds again. The crowd began to clap, and I was feeling disoriented.

"Sir, there's been a recent study that suggests a link between mental illness and tooth decay." It was Roxanne Hendley, from channel three. She was standing right in front of us, her clear eyes the color of fresh grass. Her teeth, visible beyond the amber richness of her lips, were as white and perfect as fresh snow.

"Do you believe there is any such link, and what would be its significance?"

I started resenting the way everyone was looking at me with curiosity and sympathy, like I was a damn shame. My agitation was manifested by an increased heart rate and a rise in body temperature. My colony of fleas sensed the change, reacting with excitement. They crawled, clamored, bit, chewed, mated, everywhere, all at once. I could hardly stand it, but there was nothing I could do. Not in front of Roxanne Hendley.

"Well, Ms Hendley, (Roxanne beams at the mention of her name), some truths are self-evident. Fourteen years without proper dental care is going to result in problems. Tooth decay is analogous to social decay in that both must be identified and treated or else the decay spreads, along with it's misery, throughout the system."

My resentment began to grow into anger. It wasn't even my anger, though. My anger had been perverted by humiliation. I didn't trust myself, and just watched as the anger and humiliation mixed in a toxic cloud of emotion, rising dark and churning ominously.

The clouds had moved right in on top of us. They covered the whole sky, rolling dark and low, the pressure mounting till it seemed about to smother me.

It started to rain, cold, heavy and thick. People began turning sideways, shoulders hunched, confused, the weight of the downpour disorienting everyone. The mayor stepped blindly toward me, reaching out, trying to cover his hair, confused.

Someone grabbed me. It was the Dragonfly bodyguard. He grabbed me and pushed me aside. He tossed me aside, with indifference, his concern only for the mayor.

The anger burned white hot. There was an instant, a moment before meltdown, when the intensity of the heat burned away the humiliation and the anger stood glowing pure.

I hit the son of a bitch as hard as I could right on the side of the head, and he dropped like a rock. Another wave of rain hit, like someone had messed with the volume dial.

I got lost in the rain. I just stepped back into the downpour and wandered out into the street. Traffic was all fouled up, and it was a good thing because meltdown was blurring my senses. The rain hissed, steaming off my body and fogging my sense of direction.

A maroon wave rose and carried me backward. I started to panic, tripped over a trash can, and was on my hands and knees. The rain hissed and buzzed, and I know where I am now because of all the flies. I'm up against the screen and there aren't any flies in the rec room. The flies are trying to get in, buzzing up and down, but the steel grates are in place and nobody's slashed the screens and Hank is in there, beating the Mexican kid at ping-pong.

The florescent light is shining white. It's surprising how bright and crisp everything is. I'm seeing everything new and it looks the same, the couch where a couple of manics are smoking and watching the six o'clock news, and it looks the same, except I'm outside looking in and it looks different.

Ron is pushing a mop around the pool table, trying to reach a spot way underneath. He's not really doing any good, it's just an excuse to be in the rec room, and when Hank burns a ball past the Mexican kid, Ron drops the mop and goes chasing it down the hallway. He's done it twice already, and I'm watching him. I can see down the hallway from the window, and I see Angela Blackmore step out of her office. I want to duck so she doesn't see me, but I can't seem to move and stare as the ball bounces ahead of Ron, and Angela scoops it up on a bounce. Ron skids to a stop in front of her, like a kid running out of control, and Angela smiles and gives him the ball. Ron's nodding his head and grinning like a retard and turns to run back to the rec room while Angela watches him with a smile. Then her face freezes. She doesn't recognize me at first; she just sees a face staring in the window and it startles her. I can't seem to move. My face is burning with embarrassment, but I can't move and then Angela recognizes me with relief and begins to laugh because she was startled in the first place. It's not a menace at all, it's just that idiot, Emerson. Ron looks up to see what she's laughing at, but she can't talk and just points and Ron turns and sees me and he laughs, and Hank and the Mexican kid turn and they see me in the window. Everyone's laughing now, me out against the screen with the flies. Their laughter builds and echoes down the hallway and the patients and nurses come out of the rooms and everyone's laughing and even the manics are snickering into their fists, they can't believe how stupid I look. And the worst part was, I wanted to get in as bad as the flies.

"You ok, mister?"

The rain's let up now and I can see where I'm in the alley behind Stacey's. It's a narrow alley with old orange brick on both sides and there's a fan blowing smoke and onion grease out into the air above me, humming with a low sound I took for flies.

A kid is standing there with his little sister and she's got some weeds in her hand and her brother's holding her other one. He's maybe eight or nine, and she's just a little thing with a bouquet of weeds she's picked. There's weeds growing along the orange bricks where the pavements shrunk and cracked. Dark green weeds with little blue flowers that you wouldn't even think were pretty till a little girl picks them and makes a bouquet.

"You ok, mister?" the kid asks, and I'm on my hands and knees in some wet garbage and my head is pounding. The kid's not scared or nothing, but he should be. He shouldn't even be back there. I tried to tell him, but my words come out all jumbled and don't make any sense.

"He's drunk," the little girl says, wrinkling up her nose in disgust, as though finally catching wind of me. Her coat isn't even buttoned and it's damn cold, and I tried to tell them they shouldn't be back in the alley by themselves, but I can't seem to talk and the little girl giggles. The kid asks me if I've seen his mama.

"You seen our mama, mister? She's skinny and

her name is Deloris and she ain't come home since Wednesday."

It was a terrible thing, and my guts hurt so bad I felt like someone had kicked me and I tried to get up, but when I moved my head there was an explosion of red and the pain drove deep, right down through my brain and I could only close my eyes and try to re-center myself.

"He's drunk. Let's go," the little girl said again, tugging at her brother's hand.

"You gonna be ok, mister?" the kid asks, all concerned, and I just nodded my head. It was terrible.

"You see Deloris, tell her to get her ass home, ok mister?"

They shouldn't have been back there all by themselves. It's no place for a couple of little kids. Nothing but garbage and busted glass and her coat wasn't even buttoned. But when I tried to get up, another explosion of red and my arm buckled, and I slumped against the garbage can sending it clanging across the pavement.

They turned and ran down the alley, the little girl holding onto her brother's hand and looking back at me as he led her down around the dumpster at the far end of the alley. By the time I got there, they weren't nowhere in sight. Just a little bunch of weeds on the sidewalk.

But if you see Deloris, tell her to get her ass home.

I was nervous. About hitting the Dragonfly. And about having a nervous breakdown, but I recognized the trouble with that line of thinking and quickly tried to change my direction of thought.

I need a plan.

The best thing to do would be to just disappear. I had to get off the streets for a couple days. The Dragonfly was probably still around somewhere close, and he'd be looking for me.

I decided to go see Charles. Charles could be irritating, but I was wet through and chilled and the thought of sitting in Charles' boxcar was appealing. Besides, Charles wouldn't ask how I was, and that fit my mood. So I headed north, on Third Street. Walking back down Brewery Street to the river seemed foolish. But if I went far enough north, five or six blocks, I could cut down through the warehouses and reach the riverbank without running into anyone who gave a damn about any of it.

North of the brewery was a couple of blocks of old warehouses on a low, flat plain of the valley which most people avoided. I hated walking down around the warehouses. Old, forgotten brick buildings that used to be the heart of the city—train depots and grain elevators and bank buildings that were now just used to keep the rain off obsolete typewriters and plumbing supplies. It was depressing walking down there because you could tell nobody gave a damn. Whoever owned the buildings sure as hell weren't going to be sitting in a chair out front with a smile and a wave. I bet they never even went down there anymore. Just truck drivers and security guards, and you could tell just by looking at them, they didn't want to be down there either.

Around every warehouse was a chainlink fence and signs warning against trespassing. There was one huge building, six stories high with about eight hundred windows; half of them busted out. Too high to reach them with a rock, so somebody had been up there busting windows, and it depressed the hell out of me to think about it. Probably some guy who was drunk and hating everything. Hating everything, but it was just him and he was drunk and alone and he started by throwing a bottle and probably screaming 'Fuck it' at the top of his lungs, and there was a wild shattering in the night. And he was drunk, by himself on the sixth floor of that moldy old building where everything was just left to sit and rot and nobody gave a damn about any of it. That shattering glass was the only thing he could do that seemed to matter. So he threw another bottle, and then another and anotherandanother, rapid fire, shattering glass all around him till the whole world was coming down and he couldn't stop because if he did, he'd just be drunk and alone in all that rot and pretty soon he slammed his fist into the windows because there wasn't anything left to throw and a security guard called the cops and they found him up there in a pool of his own blood, crying like a fool because nothing had changed.

They got that guy in another warehouse now, and there isn't any glass to shatter. He's in a corner somewhere, moldy and forgotten and nobody even cared enough to fix the damn windows.

Behind the biggest building was a chest high pile of creosote blackened railroad ties in which Charles had fashioned a hiding place for his old blue bike; just a little crevasse about 20 inches wide into which he could slide his bike. You wouldn't notice it unless you stood just right and looked right at it. The rear tire was just visible beyond the blackened ties, and although it were no guarrantee that Charles would be home, it gave me hope. A slow, steady rain had begun, and I was starting to shake.

Behind the pile of railroad ties a path leads down into a ravine littered with old tires and rusted filing cabinets; everything half burried in leaves and debris washed down from above. The ravine weaves down through the bluffs for about fifty yards before running up against an exposed wall of limestone. At that point, the ravine turns hard towards the river and drops off sharp and steep. Along the face of the limestone wall rising up from the ravine are carved a series of steps barely noticeable beneath a covering of leaves and moss, which lead up to the crest of the next ridge. The limestone ridge is narrow, dropping again on the far side into another ravine. From the crest, if you know where to look, you can see Charles' boxcar hidden down below in a thick stand of aspen.

Out of habit, I approached Charles' boxcar carefully and as quietly as possible. It was easy to be quiet because the leaves were wet and my footsteps were muffled. Charles hated it when I surprised him, so I usually made it a point to do so. He was home, the door of his boxcar ajar by a couple feet, and there echoed the familiar sound of his manual typewriter from within. I looked around for a suitable rock, something big enough to echo, and was about to hurl it against the steel, when it occured to me that I didn't want to piss Charles off any sooner than I inevitably would. Instead, I dropped the rock and coughed loudly.

The typewriter continued to tap, tap, tap like a brain dead woodpecker. I coughed again, louder, still with no result. It wasn't until several coughs later that the typewriter finally fell quiet.

"You sick or what?" Charles' voice echoed irritably from inside the boxcar. I picked up my rock and hurled it against the steel as hard as I could. It made a nice echo.

Charles' boxcar was cluttered with paper, the way it gets when he's working on something. He was typing another letter to the editor, an old black typeweriter perched on the table, a jar of wilted black-eyed susans pushed off to the side. Yellow sheets of typewritten paper lay everywhere and he busied himself with collecting them together as I climbed in, as though he were afraid I would pick one up and read it.

Charles was a friendly enough guy. He made me feel welcome, setting a beer on the table and laying his cigarettes right out in the open where I could see how many he had. Still, he seemed distracted. It was the nuclear waste issue eating on him. His eyes, magnified in the thick lenses, appeared tired and bloodshot, and there were lapses in the conversation, where he would simply gaze out the boxcar door at the cottonwood leaves flickering in the breeze and tearing free on the gusts, swirling down into the thick layer covering the forest floor. Charles rubbed his temples and fidgeted.

He did have a point about the danger of storing nuclear waste on the banks of the most populated waterway in the nation. Perhaps he was an alarmist, as Caeser claimed, but it was a somewhat alarming concept, to hear Charles describe it. He asked me to envision radioactive waste being released into the river and spreading down through the heartland, contaminating the water and food supply for ten thousand years.

He got us each another beer and offered me a smoke. He was a good host.

Mad as hell, though.

"It's a scandal. Everyone's living for the damn moment. The least, Emerson, the very least anyone who has the privilege of spending time on this planet should be required to learn are the basic facts of our ecosystem. I swear to you, man, half the people in this city do not understand the concept of photosynthesis, let alone the dangers of nuclear waste."

Charles was on his feet.

Photosynthesis has something to do with sunshine and the production of energy. Franklin told me, otherwise I'd never heard of it before. Although my grasp of the concept was shallow at best, I nodded my head in somber agreement, not wanting to appear ignorant. Charles was livid, pacing about the boxcar, trying to burn off his frustration. Suddenly he stopped, looking straight at me, those wild eyes tearing straight in.

"He was a fool," he said.

"You're right," I agreed.

"Regardless, you must interact to produce a moment."

I did not respond. I swear to you, Ed Ludgrin was crazy. He hung himself from the rafters of a barn he bought in South Dakota. He died a success.

"Not necessarily," Charles continued, for the sake of argument. "A man may choose the moment."

"You're right," but Charles was staring off into space and I doubt he even heard me. Which was okay with me. I wasn't even sure what I'd just agreed to. I felt sorry for Charles. His madness was reaching an apex, the climatic apex of madness. From such a height one sees for miles and the soul soars, but only briefly. The descent is often rapid and brutal. Charles was approaching meltdown.

There was nothing I could say to prevent it, and I knew Charles didn't want it prevented. He was rushing toward it with abandon, looking for a release.

So we sat and drank our beer and listened to the rustling leaves and a late litter of skunks squeaking and whining beneath the floor. The low clouds were thick and it was still raining, the sound of it strumming across the roof of the boxcar and hypnotizing me. Now and then a gust of wind sprayed misty cold and fresh through the open doorway. Charles lit a fire and brought out his checkers, and we played until it started getting dark. Charles had to go to work, and we'd finished the beer.

I had a pretty good buzz going when I left the boxcar, heading down the path toward the bridge. It was a mellow buzz, a bittersweet buzz of acceptance. I just didn't much give a damn about anything.

The rain tapered off to a fine mist, but the wind had become stronger, giving the night a wild feeling, like renegade spirits were loose and bent on raising hell, swarming through the big cottonwoods, which instinctively fought back, rustling with excitement. The trees were strong and sensible with wisdom gained only through quiet contemplation. The wind was laughing, wild and free. A wild battle overhead; the giant trees swaying and groaning as the wind mounted and bore down, the tension building till the strain filled the air, then passing with a wave and a sigh, only to begin mounting towards another assault. It was an ancient battle, and instincts stirred deep inside me. Like a broken saddle horse catching the scent of a wild herd up in the hills.

I closed my eyes and felt it, listening deep. A gust tore through the brush, rushing down the bluff and swirling around me. My clothes flapped and whipped, and I spread my arms. My mind tilted, caught an updraft, and began to lift, rising up out of the ravine, soaring into the topmost branches and still higher, riding a wild freedom. Loose and free, howling, the wind filled my senses. The rush filled my mind and was as real as the wind itself.

Then in real close, so close I could feel the warmth of its breath on my cheek, so close the warmth passed over me like a shadow, softly but with dead certainty, fear spoke.

"Fool."

A chill gripped me. I reeled backwards and stumbled to the ground, into the wet leaves and brush and the wind still howled, but it was laughing. Standing there in the darkness, laughing low at what it'd done. I couldn't move at first, I was so scared. It turned and melted into the brush, muffled footsteps in the wet leaves as it slid through the shadows. It moved up the bank, paused, then moved again.

I don't know who it was. I wanted to chase it down, to demand an explanation, but I was scared. I'd felt the warmth of its breath. We'd been standing face to face, for Christ's sake.

The wind howled. I scrambled to my feet and ran. Not after it, hell no. I ran for the bridge, stopping to catch my breath at the top of the ridge, waiting and watching and listening to see if whoever it was was following me.

I can't explain it, but I'd felt the warmth of its breath on my face.

The smell of woodsmoke drifted sweet in the air, and I slowed down, trying to re-center myself. I could hear Joe cursing. Franklin was under the bridge, and Joe was cursing his dogs.

"Get out. Get the hell out of here, you bunch of scavenging, parasitical bastards."

"Hell, Joe, they don't mean any harm. Just paying compliments to your cooking, known as the finest pigeon stew in the valley."

Clyde was investigating the stew pot, reaching out carefully with his nose, ready to dodge the stick Joe waved menacingly before him.

"They're awfully hungry, then," Caeser was saying, "For that's mighty thin soup. Mostly water, and purifying heat. We're about to sterilize the camp, Franklin. We could knock down two birds with one stone, come to think about it—dog stew and clean blankets. What'dya say?"

They jumped as I stepped around the rock, the dogs barking in surprise. "Jesus, Emerson, don't do that. Hey, what's the problem? You look like hell."

I wasn't sure. I just shrugged and sat down on the cooler.

"It's them damn fleas," Joe said, "They're making him anemic."

Franklin waved him off. "Hell, fleas won't kill you. And as far as birds go, when you enjoy the companionship of a natural bird dog, you don't need stones."

Alice stood proudly in the firelight, tail beating the air, a pigeon stuffed in her mouth. A brown and white one. The dog growled when Caeser leaned forward to get a closer look.

"It's hers. Can't fault her. It's instincts, naturally bred in. Third pigeon she's found today."

Caeser nodded. "Ain't blaming her. That's a fine bird. She's got a right to be proud."

Franklin nodded at the compliment.

"Proud or not," Joe said, scratching and looking irritated, "we're about to sterilize the camp. Anything with fleas on it goes into the pot. Dog stew it'll be, if any of these mutts gets too close." He jerked and twisted the stick up behind his back, trying to reach between his shoulder blades, muttering threats. Franklin was wise enough to retreat, heading down into the shadows below camp, his dogs chasing and yelping through the brush.

"Goddamn dogs," Joe said, throwing his stick down in disgust. "Look, Emerson, we gotta purge the camp. Let's me and you put on some of them green pajamas of yours. Caeser can boil out the fleas while we go down to the river. We gotta purge. I can't go on like this."

I was not centered. The wind blew, and my thoughts drifted with the sparks. I simply did as told, piling my infested clothing and blankets beside the fire, changing into the greens. Joe was so skinny he had to wrap his around at the waist and use a safety pin off his coat to hold them up. He handed me a length of rope, and Caeser provided us each with a plastic straw. "Cheer up, Emerson. You look like you're about to be shot."

"He'll feel better in an hour," Joe answered for me. "His blood supply is low. I can't believe Franklin lives like this. His skin must be thick as leather."

"Franklin's wired different. He accepts things." Joe snorted.

"Man accepts what he's stuck with. What sort of man accepts fleas?"

Caeser just chuckled, using Joe's stick to lower his pants into the boiling pot. We all knew the answer.

I followed Joe down the willow path. Following is an easy thing, once one accepts it. It can be done without much thought.

Down below the bank, we waited in the darkness of the ravine, watching a blue security car patrol the railyard. A spotlight swept the shadows, searching beneath the boxcars. A flash of a match, a cigarette glowed red and they passed so close to us we could hear the radio squawking, gravel popping and snapping beneath the tires. The wind gusted, swirling leaves down through the misty white light, creating little twisters that spun across the tracks, breaking apart as the leaves scattered between the rails. The patrol car looped at the north end of the yard, under the bridge, and headed south. Joe waited until they disappeared behind a line of boxcars, then told me to run and bolted out of the ravine, his greens flapping loose on his skinny frame.

The wind swirled leaves and mist across the tracks and we dodged from shadow to shadow.

Once again I found myself standing on the concrete wall, looking over the dark expanse of the river. I wasn't afraid. Not of the river. I was fear stricken. I kept waiting to hear footsteps behind me, the warmth of its breath on my neck. The wind tumbled cold and misty down from the bluffs, where fear lay hidden up in the ravines. The waves splashed up against the wall, a tangy smell in the air. A tug worked off the loading docks, its spotlight sweeping across the water. Traffic rolled across the bridge, a diesel downshifting low.

"Emerson, dammit, wake up." Joe's already stripped naked with his rope tied around his waist. "Tie your rope to the barge anchor," he's telling me, and I do but my mind's thick and it's hard to concentrate.

Suddenly, from out of the darkness, somewhere over the river, a goose started crying. Just a lone goose, flying low, its call traveling over the water with clarity and emotion. It was stunning, how clear it was in the misty air.

Joe sighed. "Poor bastard," he said. "Poor bastard lost its mate. He'll fly all night, crying for her."

We waited a minute, and the goose cried again, this time far out over the river, headed south.

"Poor bastard."

Joe got sentimental over the strangest things. He could lift two bucks off Murphy and not worry about his feelings in the least, but the sound of a lonely goose in the night softened him all up.

I started feeling sentimental too, listening to the goose way off down the valley, its cry finally fading into the mist and low grind of the augers. I was kind of emotional, anyways. Fear is an emotion. It certainly feels like one, anyways. I spoke without thinking.

"Joe," I said, "you ever been in love?"

Soon as I said it, I felt stupid. Joe didn't say anything at first. I was beginning to hope he hadn't heard me. Maybe I hadn't even spoken out loud. I was kind of messed up.

"I don't know, Emerson. Dammit, I've got fleas chewing my ass raw and if you don't mind, I'd rather drown the bastards than stand here butt naked discussing love with a dumb fuck kid."

Joe could be the most unfeeling bastard at times. I should never had asked. I wouldn't've, if I'd thought about it first. That's why a guy doesn't like to feel emotional. You always end up making an ass out of yourself. Joe must've sensed my mood. He sighed again.

"Ok. It's just a hell of a question, is all. Can't you see? You ask that goose if he's loved, and chances are he'll pick out your eyes in response. You can assume he's known love, just by his crying, and assuming is all you should do." "I'm not asking the God damn goose. It's obvious, him crying like that.

I don't have to ask him, for Christ's sake. I'm asking you. You're not flying around in the middle of the night crying lost and miserable. How the hell am I suppose to know if I don't ask?"

Then, in response, Joe starts flapping his elbows and honking sad like a lonely goose till I had to laugh and then he jumped into the river, still flapping and honking. Dysfunctional people have the strangest sense of humor. Joe was crazy, and I felt empowered by the ludicrous sight of him standing buck naked and flapping his scrawny arms and honking like an idiot, so I said the hell with it and jumped.

Only the God damn rope was too short. I had assumed the son of a bitch had given me a long enough piece of rope to reach the water, for Christ's sake.

The rope tightened on my waist like a noose, then snapped up hard into my armpits. Like a dope on a rope, I swung backwards, slamming in against the concrete wall hard, stunned, hanging there with my feet dangling in the water. My entire body was just a dull, throbbing, aching sensation. The light from the barge swept past, the rope slipped up my arms and over my head, and I slithered into the water like a dead fish.

Joe grabbed me from sinking, but I'm not giving him credit for saving my life because he's the son of a bitch who gave me the short rope in the first place. "You okay?" he kept asking, but I refused to answer at first. I was feeling disoriented. For a moment I couldn't focus and started to panic. The water was deep and the current strong, and underwater the low rumble of the tug filled my head. I felt like I was going to drown. I kept envisioning my bare ass floating down among the barges, somebody hooking a rope onto my ankle and hauling my dangling body up through the air to the barge deck, everyone standing around looking at my naked corpse flung out at their feet. Some guy would roll me over with his foot and you know one of them barge bastards would make some sort of sick joke about me.

"Settle down," Joe kept saying, then the current would pull us both under and the tug engines would hum in my head and I would panic.

"Dammit, Emerson, I'm going to let you go," Joe was threatening me. "You don't quit punching, I'm going to let you go."

I quit punching. Joe sounded serious, and the last thing I wanted was them barge bastards hauling me out in the morning.

"Okay. Can you climb?" Joe asked. "If you can't climb, I'm going to let your ass go, 'cause there's no other way out of here, and I'll be damned if I'm going to drown just to keep you company."

After about a miserable hour in the river, I was able to climb up on Joe's shoulders, reach my rope, and pull myself up the concrete wall. I had to help Joe up, he was worn out from holding onto me. We both lay there. Joe was puking.

There is nothing like a near death experience for arousing a mixture of conflicting emotions. I dared not speak for fear I would begin to laugh about it. Sometimes it's hard to be angry. Sometimes I think the angriest people in the world are just mad because they can't laugh because if they do, nobody will take them seriously. Of course, my anger was pointless, as far as Joe was concerned.

I had to almost drag him back across the railroad tracks. He stumbled and leaned against me, head down and breathing heavy, chills convulsing his body. I started feeling responsible in a way, for he'd spent himself holding onto me in the water. Instead of giving him hell for the short rope, I struggled against a developing sense of gratitude. Of course, that's probably what his plan was. Joe was the sneakiest bastard I've ever met.

The brush and trees along the willow path were covered with drops of water, now and then the wind gusting and shaking loose a shower. The path was muddy and slippery, seemingly steeper in the dark, winding and back weaving and I began to wonder if it was even the right damn trail.

It was a relief to catch the first scent of our campfire. The smell of woodsmoke was sweet. The thought of our clean clothes drying on the rocks produced a domestic feeling of reassurance.

It was short lived, however, this domestic feeling of reassurance. I did not immediately comprehend the change. The sweet smell of woodsmoke turned sour, the acrid smell of black, thick smoke now hung in the air. I hesitated, trying to decipher its meaning. Joe, however, immediately came to life.

"The son of a bitch," he said, "The son of a bitch is burning our clothes." He pushed past me, sprinting up the path. I could hardly keep up.

Caeser was asleep in his chair, head rolled back and his mouth open, completely oblivious to the black smoke billowing from the stew pot not ten feet away from him. He sprang to his feet when he heard us, dazed and useless. Joe kicked the pot off the fire, and the remnants of my corduroy suit scattered across the ground, the charred pieces glowing red along the edges. None of the pieces were larger that a square foot, but I stomped on them anyways, mostly out of frustration. Caeser helped me, feeling guilty, I suppose, but Joe realized his clothes were draped safely over the blue rock, warm and dry, and began to dress himself, no longer concerned. I don't blame him. It was obvious there was no chance of saving anything. Caeser and I stompeduntil the charred pieces were reduced to black scraps and ashes.

Using a stick, Caeser held up a longer piece of charred material, black and crusty. It was either a pants leg or a coat sleeve. Either way, it no longer mattered.

"Damn sorry, Emerson," Caeser apologized, but I refused to accept it. I was disgusted, filled with self-righteous anger. I had a right to be angry and capitalized on it. I glorified in it. Snatching a dry blanket from a nearby rock, draping it dramatically around my shoulders, I sat angrily on the cooler and stared bitterly into the fire, refusing to utter a word of forgiveness or even open the door to peace by acknowledging him in any way. I became a fortress of resolve.

There was tension in the air. Caeser tried to say something funny about dehydrated fleas, but I refused to laugh, and Joe didn't dare to. He sat quietly examining his toes through a hole in his sock for the thousandth time that summer.

Caeser sighed, got up from the chair, and without a word, wandered off down into the willows. Neither Joe nor I acknowledged his absence or his return a few minutes later. I was starting to calm down, though.

Caeser sauntered up, all humble, and dropped a quart of whisky into my lap, three quarters full. Joe's mouth hung open. I couldn't believe it either. We were both thinking the same thing.

"That's all there is, dammit." Caeser read our minds. "You two can tear those willows out by the roots if you want, but that's all I've got down there. And it's yours Emerson. Damn sorry about your clothes. You just drink it yourself and don't bother sharing it with a couple of bums like us. We don't deserve it."

Joe nodded his head in agreement. "You're damn right. Neither of us deserve a drink. You just get drunk on your own."

They were playing me for a sucker, but I didn't mind anymore. Joe offered me a cigarette, and if I were really mad, I would've refused, but I wasn't so I took it. But no one was talking. They just sat staring thoughtfully at the fire while I caught a buzz.

Eventually, the alcohol ate away my resolve, like they knew it would. Resolve is soluble in alcohol. I struggled to maintain my impassive silence, but it wasn't natural. They did not speak, but simply waited.

Finally, I began to talk, like they knew I would, and they nodded and agreed with everything I said.

"Looks like it might rain all night." I said, just to get things going. "Yes, I believe you're right, Emerson. It does seem to be settling in."

We sat poker faced. Joe poked absently at the snapping fire. Overhead, the storm grates rattled with the passing traffic.

"Traffic's light for it being so early."

Caeser looked thoughtful, running a hand over his beard, gazing up at the bridge.

"It is early."

Joe nodded his head solemnly. "Damn unusual."

The wind gusted, swirling sparks, bearing down from the north cool and unfriendly, and I said it was blowing from the south but neither argued. I said the train down below was carrying soybeans when we knew it was carrying corn, but neither tried to contradict me. I said the fire needed more wood and without a word of ridicule, Joe threw three more sticks on it, even though it was burning fine and it was just a waste of wood. So I said they were a couple of bastards, and they both solemnly agreed. Then I apologized for calling them bastards because the whisky was making me mellow and offered them a drink to make it up and they refused at first, and I started getting mad again so they both quickly gave in and took a drink and we started passing the bottle around and soon we were cursing and laughing and Joe was describing me dangling on the end of the rope and Caeser was laughing so hard he rolled his chair over backwards.

The fire burnt low, sparks rolling off on the breeze and spinning around the rocks. The traffic was light now, and as it grew late we grew quiet and each drew into himself, comfortably and without awkwardness. The lonely goose passed up the valley, mourning soulfully; its lonely cry like a spirit from the dark mist over the river. A beautiful, bluesy sound; like a gutsy, raw sax in the night.

"Poor bastard," Joe said, quiet, at the fire, and Caeser and I nodded without speaking. All three of us were sentimental then, with the warmth of the whisky and the warmth of the fire and companionship and a moment came where there was acceptance. And with the acceptance came contentment. Simple contentment, and everything seemed to fall into place, easy and right.

Then I'll be damned if the mayor doesn't show up again.

All of a sudden there's people coming down the park path. Shouts and laughter and a light flickers, dances across the willows, then slams into us with blinding intensity, washing away the night and even the fire is just a pile of grey, smoking ashes. The three of us sat stunned.

Caeser and Joe bolted out of their chairs, froze in the spotlight, a look of confusion and alarm on their faces. Then, in unison, they ducked and disappeared down into the shadows of the willows below camp. It was instinct, pure and simple. Instincts which my institutionalized life had not developed in me. Coupled with the whisky shorting out my nervous system, I had not even gotten off the cooler before they were out of sight.

"Hello! Don't be alarmed! It's just me, Al Mckinnley, your mayor and representative. Hello! Don't run!"

I had barely made it to my feet before I was locked in a handshake with the mayor in the face of three tv cameras and half a dozen reporters with microphones held out towards me. The lights were blinding, and I could only see the red dots of the cameras flickering and the mayor's smile, bright teeth and frozen hair and he's pumping my arm and wants to know my name and the last time I'd been to a dentist. The lights are bright and it's hard to see and I've got my greens on and the Mayor doesn't recognize me as the same guy he'd shaken hands with earlier in the day. I was surprised and couldn't think straight.

"Eleven years!" the mayor exclaimed, "Eleven years since Mr Whitebird has seen a dentist!" and he went on to give a speech about the injustice of the system and the need for reform and the prevalence of tooth decay in the homeless population of the city.

The mayor had a big cottonwood leaf stuck to his hair. Just stuck there, on top of his head, curled up like a ribbon or flower. A big one, so you'd think he had to know about it. I didn't say anything, and tried to just ignore it. Still, I wonder how long it stuck there, and who finally said something about it.

What really bothered me were the bright lights and the fact that I couldn't see the Dragonfly. I started feeling nervous about it. Latent instincts began to awaken, warning me to run, but the mayor had a firm grip on my hand. Luckily, my hands sweat when I get nervous. It's usually embarrassing. I usually avoid even shaking hands when I'm nervous. I waited, collecting my thoughts, my hand starting to sweat like crazy, and just as the mayor started speaking of festering wounds, I wrenched it free, ducked my head and bolted for the willows.

Ramming my head square into the middle of the Dragonfly's chest. He had snuck up behind me, and I'm sure revenge was on his mind. But he must've been blinded by the lights and never saw me coming. Knocked off balance, he started tap dancing frantically backwards over the wet rocks. His fingers brushed the front of my greens, missed their grip, and he sailed over backwards, landing with a curse flat on his back. I jumped over him and headed for the willows while the mayor tried to reassure me.

"Please, don't be alarmed! Hello!"

The brightness of the lights hardened the shadows of the riverbank— pushed them back, concentrating them down in the willows and below in the ravines, crouching low and waiting. I ran with abandon, my motivation just and subconciously approved. I did not fear the darkness, but the bright lights which shone with such unnatural intensity. The darkness was a cool balm for my anxiety, and as my anxiety faded, my confidence grew.

Bright light fools. You are dared to follow me into the darkness of my realm.

The willows whipped, spraying cold rainwater, the cotton greens soaked cool, tight against my skin. Alive and alert, I reached the crest of the railyard and headed south, downriver on the bum trail, my feet instinctively falling where expected, over logs and washouts, free of fear or hesitation. Disdainful of pursuit, confident in my ability to navigate the uncertainty of darkness. Dodging on instincts, running on faith.

Instincts are based on routine much as confidence is based on familiarity. The wind had blown the rotted torso of an old elm across the path. It was not in my data base. It clipped me at the knees and sent me hurtling head over heels down into the turtle pond ravine.

I rolled forward, suspended weightless, filled with dread at the sickening loss of equilibrium, anticipating oblivion at any instant, the rush of air and the intense darkness, pitch black to an obscure depth.

A flash of bright red and the frogs were chirping. Sunk heavy in wet leaves, pressed flat, numb and thick. No wind, no rush, just the bright red chirping of the frogs, from every angle, saturating the air. And the sound of my heartbeat, muffled, thumping dull and distant, as though emanating from somewhere out in the darkness of the ravines.

As I lay there, dazed and thick, a sense of presence began to form. The abstract feeling of being watched ran up my neck like a spider. I saw it at the same moment it spoke, low and certain.

"Fool."

In the depths of the ravine, a darker shade of black, like a shadow between the massive trunks of the cottonwoods, it reached for me. Fear gripped my soul, ripped free the confidence, and dropped it on the ground at my feet, bleeding and bruised, writhing in the wet leaves.

"Who are you?" I stammered, shocked by the severity of the wound. "I am what you fear." It spoke flat, dead, and certain. "Hang on."

Suddenly the wind gusted, like a great wall of water rushing down through the ravine. The ground rolled with the cascading sound of the cottonwoods, loose and wild and the wind swept me away, swirling and tumbling, lost and helpless, all sense of balance and bearing obliterated in the cascading river of wind and sound.

Tired. Exhausted. Bruised and sore. But for the beating of my heart, silence. Above, the sky had cleared, the stars shining bright. Brighter and closer than I'd ever seen them. Thousands, clear and crisp, with no end to it, just a vastness of stars that went on forever.

My thoughts expanded and raced across the universe. Mesmerized, I stared at the stars and thought about God. I'm not going to tell you what I thought because you'd think I was preaching, but nobody knows how big the universe is, and that's a simple truth.

Having expanded, my thoughts came back together in a chaotic mess. Just getting off the ground was awkward. My legs felt distant, my arms distracted. I was unsure of myself. The frog's chirping, swirling in from every angle, so permeated the darkness as to become an aspect of silence. There was a knot on my head, my neck stiff and sore. It concerned me. It was stupid, but I kept thinking about Ron, my old roommate, and his cousin.

Ron told me his cousin was riding a mule in the Grand Canyon and a bee stung the mule and it threw his cousin, who landed on his head. I don't remember the guy's name, but Ron said he was fine until he went to sleep that night. He had a concussion, and didn't wake up for twelve years. He just laid there, and someone had to brush his teeth. Ron said his mom used to take him to visit his cousin and make him talk to the guy, who just laid there, drooling on his pillow. The thought of Ron talking to me while I laid there drooling just bothered the hell out of me. And Ron would do it, I was sure of it. And maybe I'd be able to hear him, but there'd be no way to tell him to shut up. For twelve years. It was stupid, but it bothered me.

My heart was still pounding plain, as though coming from out of the darkness around me, a slow, two beat rhythm. Amazed, I put my hand on my chest, then realized the sound and my heart were not synchronized. Franklin was busy stomping beer cans. The sound carried easily through the still, cool air, audible from two hundred yards away. I decided to go see Franklin. He'd have a fire and a pot of coffee.

With no breeze to carry my scent, and the monotony of Franklin's can smashing having lulled the dogs to sleep, I was standing beside the fire before anyone noticed me. Franklin's dogs hated to be surprised. They jumped up and barked like fools, only Clyde and Sadie, though. Alice wasn't around, and that was strange because she usually wanted me to scratch her ears all the time. Franklin hardly missed a beat. He went on crushing cans as though I'd been standing there all night. He hated to be surprised as much as the dogs, but hated admitting it even worse. I asked him about Alice.

"Don't feel well. It's all them pigeons she's been eating. Pigeon meat is strong. Full of amino acids. Takes a lot of energy to digest it. She's in the weeds, digesting."

I remembered the pigeon lying in the gutter up on Brewery Street, the brown and white one. He paused, absently scratching his head.

"Damn peculiar that it should be another brown and white one, Emerson." I didn't say anything. Franklin had his own way of looking at things. The brown and white ones were kind of special to me, I just didn't like to see them lying around dead. Nothing peculiar about it.

Franklin set up two more cans, stomped each, kicked them aside, and grabbed two more from the pile beside him. He spoke as he moved, repeating the same motions over and over.

"How come you're wearing those pajamas?"

I explained the short rope fiasco and how Caeser had burned my clothes. "Hell, fleas won't kill you, but the cure might. Throw some wood on the fire and dry yourself out."

Franklin was all right. There was a busted-up oak pallet laying beside the fire ring, and nothing makes a finer fire. He made some coffee, and I was soon feeling better. But sleepy. I told Franklin about hitting my head and wondering about a concussion.

"Sounds like you had a rough night. That's a hell of a lump on your head. Could be you're fine, could be you're not. The brain's a funny thing. I'm not going to tell you it's safe to go to sleep, son. Wouldn't want to burden myself. But I will say that you're gonna go to sleep, that's as sure as the sun coming up in another hour. So don't let it bother you too much. But if you do wake up to a sunny morning, you better learn to appreciate it. If I were you, I'd start thinking about all them fine mornings you took for granted and wasted away, mad at the world, and start praying for one more, and the chance to appreciate it like a man should."

I resented the hell out of it. Franklin was taking advantage of my predicament to deliver a sermon. And if I didn't wake up, his words might torment me for eternity. Suddenly it felt like I was in a hell of a fix. I resolved to stay awake until the sun rose, feel the warmth and give thanks, before drifting off into oblivion.

Franklin chuckled as I refilled my cup with coffee.

"That's right. Help yourself to the whole pot. If you can stay awake long enough to finish it."

I didn't answer. I ignored him. I didn't say anything or move until Franklin and his dogs, the two of them, had left for an early round of scavenging up in the streets. As soon as he was gone, though, I got up and did some jumping jacks.

The sky above the eastern bank was glowing brighter, pink and yellow, and the robins were starting to sing. It was the best hour for sleep, but I resisted it. Every now and then I'd get up and do some jumping jacks, just to get my metabolism going. I tried counting, trying to keep track of time, but this made the minutes seem ridiculously long. You want to live forever? Get your ass in a bind and then start counting down the minutes it takes to get out of it. Repeat until you go crazy. I skipped doing the jumping jacks once, lost count of the minutes, and to my relief, woke up to a gloriously sunny morning. The sunshine felt friendly warm, the air washed clean. It sparkled. The dew on the leaves sparkled. Red winged blackbirds perched on the chainlink fence, singing clear and fresh. Everything was so clean and fresh, I had to laugh.

I sat in Franklin's lawn chair, feeling good. From

out of the weeds, a dragonfly flitted in and landed on my knee, its lacy wings catching the sun, shining purple and green. The two of us relaxed in the sunshine, not a care in the world.

The dragonfly flew off, and I felt so good I jumped up and did some more jumping jacks, dancing around the fire ring, whooping a few times for the sheer pleasure of it. Just the clean, crisp air and the early sun and the green smells so tangy it feels wild.

There was a whimper and a rustle in the weeds and Alice hobbled out, listing sideways. She looked like hell, her sad eyes apologizing and asking for help. After a few steps forwards, she stopped and just wagged her tail, not even raising it much.

She was sick as hell, licking my hand and wimpering as I scratched her ears. Her eyes got hopeful and I talked awhile, trying to be reassuring. Worms, is what I was thinking. Franklin was going to have to save some money for medicine, and that'd probably take two weeks. Joe had some money, the couple bucks he'd lifted off Murphy. He wouldn't like the idea of spending anything on the dog, though. He blamed the dogs for the flea problem.

I started feeling disgusted with myself. It was pathetic. A twenty-four year old man ought to be able to buy medicine for a sick dog. Alice deserved better. I was just being a bum. It was time. I decided right there to move up the social ladder. Time to get a job. Maybe at the brewery. Murphy could put in a good word for me. There were always guys quitting the eleven to seven shift, always a few new faces standing around Rose's station wagon. I decided to ask Murphy about it.

I patted Alice's head and left her standing there, sad-eyed, but I felt good. Once I'd made up my mind to get a job, all sorts of possibilities appeared on my horizons. I'd get an apartment. I'd take a shower and shave and get a haircut and buy some clean clothes and come sauntering up with a hardhat and lunchbox and buy a fresh bismark, wink, and ask Rose to go to the fair or something.

The sun had climbed higher and a breeze was making the aspen leaves flutter. Dragonflies darted over the weeds, and a flock of yellow butterflies huddled around the mudpuddle. They swirled around my legs as I walked through them, being careful not to step on any. The warm sun loosened my joints, and without hardly thinking, I whooped and took off, sprinting up the bank, pushing hard and pumping my arms and leaping up the steep incline, dancing over the roots. My heart pounded wild. I felt I could've run forever. Endorphines. My brain was squirting endorphines all over the place. I felt giddy and when I reached the top of the bank, I didn't want to stop but instead did some jumping jacks, spinning around and jumping with my arms over my head before dropping into the weeds, gasping in embarrassment.

Joe and Caeser were standing there, not thirty feet up the path.

After the initial shock, they broke into spontaneous laughter. They were delighted to see me make an ass of myself, it so rarely happened. Unlike themselves, who did it on a regular basis, thus the novelty of them jackasses having worn off.

The only reason I chose to forgive them was because Caeser had a rabbit, limp and fresh. He carried it by the hind legs, flopping and bouncing from his upraised hands as he re-enacted my expression of joy. I no longer placed an absolute emphasis on pride, being neither lucky nor dumb enough. I was hungry, and pride is a luxury enjoyed on a full stomach. But there are times when I'd prefer to be the only person in paradise, where an expression of joy would not be ridiculed. It'd probably be lonely, though.

Caeser continued to harass me as I followed them up the path toward the bridge, pirouetting up in front with the rabbit flopping over his head. I refused to let it bother me. It was irritating, but the best thing to do was let Caeser make an ass of himself until he grew tired of it. Finally, Joe provided a chance to change the subject.

"Did you stick around to see what our visitors wanted last night?"

I told him it was the mayor, and Caeser heard me and quit clowning. "What the hell did he want?"

I told him the mayor was wondering about my teeth.

Joe snorted. "Same thing he was asking Franklin about. Must be considering a change of career."

Caeser struck a pose, chest out and a finger pointed at the sky. "Concerned citizenry," he began, "Some of you may be wondering why

I chose to give today's speech while holding onto a dead rabbit. It's a simple thing, folks—I thought it would help me get elected. Why the hell else would I do it?"

Except for a few red 'Vote for the Mayor' buttons and a scattering of cigarette butts, the media had left our camp undisturbed. Even the bottle, still a quarter full, lay untouched beside the cooler.

The mood was festive. There was damn near half a pack of smokes laying around. And rabbit stew. Rocking a rabbit is difficult. I've never come more than close to hitting one. Nineteen times in twenty, Joe would've missed too. A rabbit's foot is a lucky charm, and when Caeser held forth the animal, I accepted, handling it in admiration, feeling lucky. A lucky man enjoys rabbit stew.

Enjoying the atmosphere, I decided not to tell Joe and Caeser about my decision to get a job, not when it was such a nice day and everyone was feeling so good. I felt a little guilty about it. About rejecting the vagrant lifestyle, I mean, thinking they might take it personally. I wanted to enjoy the stew, just wanted to enjoy the day. A day or two wouldn't matter anyways. There were always guys quitting the late shift.

Joe had the rabbit skinned, quartered and floating in a pot of water within minutes. He had two potatoes, which he sliced in, along with a sprinkling of salt and chives. We stared at the pot, beseeching it to boil.

"Damn, I'm hungry. I could eat the whole works myself. That's the problem with wild rabbits—they're just puny. Too nervous to ever really get fat, I suppose."

"Yeah, and none of us are going to get fat off a one puny rabbit stew, even with the potatoes. I'm hungry myself. What do you say, Emerson? Feel like setting some snares?"

Snaring pigeons did not appeal to me. But a couple of pigeons would thicken the broth, and it was more an obligation of mine rather than a choice. If I wanted to eat, that is.

"Maybe just three or four," Caeser said as he handed me a small spool of fishline. "I'm not sure, but the numbers seem to be down. It's probably dispersal. The flock disperses after the last brood leaves the nest. But no sense in over doing it. Winter is coming, and the flock will need the strength."

It had been a wet night, and even though the sun was shining, the steel was cool and wet and slippery with pigeon crap. Nothing is slipperier than pigeon crap on wet steel, and I had to be careful.

It was a beautiful day, though, and as I climbed higher though the bridge, the good feeling returned to me. The air was clear and crisp. The flock felt good, and it was active, swarming over the loading docks and circling over the valley. The summer's broods were wasted on endorphines, dare-deviling up the cliffs, dive bombing each other, over emphasizing every twist and dip of the flock. Snaring is easiest on days like that, when the birds fly for the sheer pleasure of it. I felt a little guilty.

Pigeons are naive, in a way. They trusted me at fifty feet in the air. Some were almost tame, usually a youngster who'd watched me climb past its nest all summer. I never grabbed a tame bird, though. It would've seemed unsportsman like to do so.

While setting the snares, I came across a tame bird. It was a mottled pigeon, mostly grey but with brown and white feathers peppered all over its body. It was a striking bird, but listless, and it hardly blinked as I lifted it out of the way and set it on a ledge off to the side. It didn't seem hurt, just tired as hell. It was a real beauty, though, and a compliment to the flock. I would've liked to've had a whole flock of mottled pigeons like that.

The snares were set and there was nothing to do but get comfortable and wait. It was enjoyable as hell. I decided that after getting a job at the brewery, I'd still come down on the weekends and climb the bridge with Caeser. He'd let me collect for him. Even snaring wasn't so bad on a nice day. The breeze was fresh, the sunshine warm. Shades of yellow spread up the valley, and here and there a maple was burning scarlet. A raft of barges moved slowly down the middle of the river, everything slow and easy—relaxing. There wasn't any need to act like anything up there. The valley stretched out below me, and it was clear to see so much further than on the ground.

Someone was coming down the red rock path. He appeared in a clearing here, between bushes there, walking deliberately. Charles was a very deliberate guy when it came to walking. He walked to get somewhere and was not much interested in the walk itself. Flowers and red-winged blackbirds did not attract his attention. One thing to be said about Charles, he was focused.

He was free to choose, and this made him predictable—he chose madness over complacency.

He usually had smokes, though, and often brought beer, and Joe and Caeser usually greeted him with friendship. Besides, Caeser liked to argue as much as Charles. Their arguments soared under the right conditions. It was entertaining as hell, sometimes.

As I thought, there was something in the newspaper Charles carried that had offended him. He held it up as he approached, but it was too far for me to hear what he was saying. He'd done the same thing so many times that Joe and Caeser never even bothered to read the paper themselves, and just let Charles rant about it while they worked a smoke off him. That's why I was surprised to see them both get out of their chairs and crowd in close beside Charles, not even hitting him up for a smoke. Then, to my dismay, Joe and Caeser looked up at me and started laughing.

I resented the hell out of it. They were laughing straight at me. Joe, with his big, toothless grin and Caeser guffawing like an idiot. Charles was scowling deep and looking disgusted.

"A celebrity!" Caeser was crowing, "Emerson, you made the front page again!"

Before I had time to think of a proper response, a wave of pigeons hit, coming through the bracework like feathered rockets, wings popping and landing all around me. I'd been distracted and hadn't noticed them approaching from downriver. Two snagged right away, the fishline cut sharp, and their bodies fluttered down into the willows. Joe already had his sack and was chasing after them.

I hadn't yet moved, and a second wave hit. There must've been forty birds shooting in, pratically landing on top of me, their red eyes blinking blankly as they strutted the I-beams. I snared another pigeon with a clean decap and watched Joe searching the willows for it. Snared pigeons flutter a lot and it's usually pretty easy to find them.

It was not long before the next wave returned from the loading docks. They rose swarming, about thirty birds. Organizing themselves, they swept over the water and then back in along the bluffs, catching an updraft and gaining elevation. They moved as a unit, flying the same route they'd taken all summer. At sixty yards, they started dropping, building momentum. Then, in unison, they arched up and came shooting straight at me, streaking in through the steel webbing, their wings popping open like parachutes.

I snagged two more, but the second one wasn't a clean decap. It was a grey, struggling frantically against the fishline, scratching and flapping and spooking the rest of the flock until there were birds flying everywhere. It was the furthest snare out, about forty feet away, and while climbing toward it I wasn't watching my hands and reaching out, I knocked the mottled bird from its roost. I know it was the same bird because as it dropped, the brown and white flashed in the sunshine. I felt bad about it. It was dying anyways, I suppose, but falling must have been terrible.

The snared bird required two bounces. Bouncing birds is not a pleasant thing. I'd had enough of snaring by then.

Joe already had the pigeons in the pot by the time I climbed down. Pigeons are scrawny and rabbit tastes better, but Ceaser claimed you could starve on a steady diet of rabbit. Not enough nutrients, he said. But the dark meat of pigeons is loaded with protein and iron.

He was probably lying, though. Caeser was biased when it came to pigeons. He was the Pigeon Master, Master of the Flock.

The big joke in the newspaper was a picture of me and the mayor standing at the intersection up on First Street, right before the rain. He's got his arm around me, smiling bright, and I've got this dumb, fakey grin on my face and right behind us, over my shoulder, is the Dragonfly, with his dark glasses and flattop haircut, looking annoyed. The caption below read:

Mayor Mckinnley Brings comfort to the Brewery Distict. And the story below the picture was headlined:

Mental Illness and Tooth Decay; Is there a solution?

I resented the hell out of it. Joe and Caeser thought it was funny as hell.

Charles was as mad as me, but he had his own form of madness.

"Can you believe this charade?" He shook the paper at us, his eyes wide in his glasses. "The future of the entire river valley is at stake, the greatest waterway in the nation, and that son of a bitch is down here promising to fix Emerson's teeth."

I did not resent Charles. At least he wasn't laughing at me, which was more than could be said for the other two. They kept passing the picture back and forth, laughing excesssively and making jokes about my friend the mayor and how stupid I looked.

Charles settled down against the blue rock and pulled out two pints of whisky from his jacket pocket, one on either side, passing one to me and opening the other with a sharp twist, snaking down a long, drawn out shot. Charles was buzzed by the time he opened his eyes. Caeser chuckled.

"Looks like you aim to get drunk, Charles."

Charles simply nodded, took another long draw, then passed the bottle to Joe. There was a lull in the conversation as the bottles rotated a few rounds. Like the stew, a good conversation begins with a simmer. We were simmering. I chased a flea up into an armpit, and Caeser noticed.

"Dammit, Emerson, are you infested again?"

It could not be denied. At least one flea had survived the short rope purge. "That's all it takes," Joe said, "Fleas are self-pollinating. It's them damn dogs. Franklin's gotta do something about it. It's a damn health hazard." I

remembered the black dog and told them about it. "Looked tired as hell," I said.

"It's all them roadkills," Joe was poking at the fire. "Nothing worse for getting worms than eating raw roadkills. It just isn't sanitary."

The conversation swung low, into a discussion of intestinal parasites and raw meat.

"Raccoon are the worst," Caeser explained. "They're related to pigs." I did not see the connection, but it mattered little.

"Pigs will eat raw meat," Joe commented. "They'll eat anything. Must be why they call them pigs."

"That's why they've got worms, though." "Pigs are smarter than dogs."

"Hard to believe. They don't make bacon out of dogs."

"That's because pigs are so damn ugly. Nobody can love a pig."

"I had a cousin who had a pet pig. Trained it to fetch a ball. Annie or Julie or something."

"The pig or your cousin?" "I don't remember."

Loud guffaws. It was completely pointless, but it was entertaining.

The stew began a soft boil, the smell of chives and woodsmoke mixing warm and friendly. The days were getting shorter; the sun had already swung low and the valley was in shadows. The traffic was light; now and then a diesel shifted across the bridge. The augers were quiet; everyone had gone home to their families. A cool evening breeze had begun to blow. My greens were cool, but by moving closer to the fire I was able to stay warm. Charles sat brooding. He no longer passed his bottle, but kept it to himself. Joe and Caeser and I passed the other two in a crescent, back tracking and criss-crossing until no one knew whose turn it was at which bottle, or cared. We didn't say anything about Charles bogarting his bottle. For one thing, it was his, and for another, he looked mean.

"C'mon, Charles, lighten up." Caeser tried to snap him out of it. "Don't let a little radioactive contamination ruin your day."

Me and Joe were laughing at anything by now. Nuclear waste seemed hilarious. Charles looked up, but his eyes weren't huge and bulging in his glasses. They were mean little slits, and the magnification of the lenses made them seem intense. Charles was dangerously drunk.

"You can laugh," he said, talking low and direct, squinting around at us. "Go ahead, party on people. But your laughter does not alter the truth. And the truth is shameful."

Caeser was not about to back off now. He and Charles irritated the hell out of each other when they were drinking.

"Depends on which truth you're talking about, doesn't it?"

Joe sighed and poked at the fire. We both knew Charles and Caeser were going to argue.

"That's right. Let's play with logic, shall we?" Charles sat up straight, cross legged, jutting his jaw out at Caeser, his veins bulging. "You sit here laughing at the misery of future generations. It's abstract. It's not real because it's not part of your own small sense of reality. And I cannot argue with you, because your truths are limited to your own sense of reality. I feel good, therefore everything is fine. Party on, people. To hell with it."

Charles was glaring, leaning forward, daring Caeser to speak. Of course, Caeser had to say something. He could not let Charles have the last word.

"Hell, Charles, it ain't that I can't see it. It's just that I admit my insignificance, dammit. I'm just a bum, a drunk bum. I'd like to save the world, but I just don't feel up to it."

Charles was hot.

"That's a cheap excuse. We're not talking politics. Anyone of us is free to say something, to do something about the greed. We are here, alive, now. And now is the time to act. There is no excuse for not acting. Sure, you'll fail if you act. So let's avoid failure, shall we? Let's not act, and feel good about ourselves. Party on, people."

Charles took another hit off the bottle. A vicious hit. There was no pleasure in it. He emptied the bottle, coughed rough and threw the bottle at the fire, a shower of sparks dancing up into the night. I tried to follow them, but Charles' intensity drew my attention back. He climbed to his feet, leaning against the rock for support, coughing. Caeser could not let it be.

"And what are you going to do about it?"

Charles leaned back, rolling his head and staring up the valley. The stars were out, the brighter ones shining through the city haze. Most of the big dipper was visible, tilting down towards the north end of the valley. It was dripping truth.

"I'm going to shoot the mayor." Charles said, looking up the valley.

An awkward silence followed. I felt a little sorry for Caeser. He had started it. Joe sighed and stirred the stew, the smell growing richer as the meat began to cook.

"C'mon, Charles," Caeser said, quiet and friendly now, like trying to talk a guy down from a tenth story ledge. "What good would that do?"

Charles shrugged his shoulders, still leaning against the rock and staring up the valley.

"None, maybe. A little, hopefully. Look, I had

a dream last night. We were in nuclear waste land. I caught a fish, a huge carp, maybe forty pounds, but when I stuck my knife into it, black muck oozed out, and I got sick. And the pigeons. There were dead pigeons everywhere, rotting and stinking in the sun. And big flies, hairy flies, swarming everywhere, crawling all over everything and you couldn't get away from it. Flies crawling all over and buzzing till it drove me nuts."

He looked around at each of us in turn, his eyes calm now, tired, magnified by those damn glasses. "I went crazy."

No one said anything. The pigeons were restless, flapping around in the dark and cooing watery. That and the fire crackling were the only sounds.

"Any of you guys know where I can buy a gun?"

"Okay. That's enough of that talk." Joe was on his feet, but instead of facing Charles, like he was going to do, he thought the better of it and instead poked at the fire, shaking his head and muttering.

Charles' shoulders sagged apologetically.

"Yeah, you're right. Man's got to try a thing like this on his own. Accept full responsibility and limit the excuses to himself. I shouldn't have said anything."

Charles staggered across the firelight. The three of us stared at him in confusion. He disappeared into the shadows, rustling loud in the brush, having trouble finding the path. Caeser had to have the last word.

"Charles, don't be a fucking idiot."

But a diesel was coming down across the bridge, downshifting and rattling storm grates, and I don't think Charles even heard him.

"The man's an idiot." Caeser had wonder in his voice, as though a true idiot were a rare thing. He looked out in the direction Charles had taken.

"My God, I believe he intends on shooting the mayor. And I've got half a mind to let him try it. For two reasons: the mayor keeps pestering us, and Charles will only shoot himself in the foot, anyways."

Joe disagreed.

"There'll be lot's of folks mad about it. They might associate us with Charles. We'll get run right out of here."

"Perhaps our innocence has already been compromised." "Not if we don't say anything."

"Guilt by association. We're all bums."

"Ok, ok," Caeser held up his hands, "Let's not over react. Charles was drunk, as drunk as we've ever seen him. It may have just been the whisky talking. With any luck, there will be a monumental disaster of some kind in the next couple of days and Charles will refocus."

"He should have never said anything about it." Joe was disgusted. "What sort of assassin goes around talking about his business like that?"

"Charles isn't an assassin, for crying out loud. The man hardly even eats meat."

"What has that got to do with it?"

"Vegetarians are not killers. Vegetables render you pacific." "What?"

"Pacific. Charles is a pacific."

"That's pacifist. It renders you passive, you moron." "Charles is a fanatic."

"He was in Vietnam. He's killed already."

"He was younger. Thirty years of vegetables has changed his brain chemistry."

"He's crazy. A crazy man is liable to do anything."

"Ok, ok," Caeser held up his hands again. "What do you think we should do?"

None of us could think of a solution to Charle's madness, so we decided to eat. The stew was ready, and it was getting late.

Despite the impact Charles' proclamation had on the evening, once the stew was served, we managed to reach a certain level of contentment. For a hungry man will not talk while he is eating, and if no one talks, there is no arguing.

The combination of whisky and a full stomach put each of us into a mellow mood. The traffic was light, the crickets were singing, and the bats dipped through the firelight. We ate till the pot was empty, then one by one we went to roll up for the night. It was cool, and it felt good to lay under the blankets and let the crickets sing me to sleep.

Sleep came quickly to me, deep and profound. It soon became a troubled sleep, though, despite my exhaustion. I'll be damned if I didn't have Charles' dream.

I was fishing down by the power plant. I had a length of fishline and was feeling a carp running along the bottom with the bait. There wasn't enough line to let it run far. There was only another couple feet on the spool. I had to set the hook, so I jerked and the fish turned out for the middle of the river. It was a big fish, and the line cut into my fingers. It was exciting to have such a big fish struggling, its energy humming along the line. The hook was set good, but it was only a six pound test and the trick was to tire it out before pulling it in. Slowly, I waded out into the river, waiting for the fish to tire, the line stretched tight and thin, and we sat there a moment, just a steady pull, then suddenly the line went slack.

I was sure the fish was gone. Disappointed, I started winding in the line, but there was a weight on it. Dead weight. I kept winding and pretty soon the big carp floats up to the surface, white belly flashing in the sunshine.

I pulled it up on shore, a two foot carp with no marks of any kind on it. It'd just died. The fish looked okay to eat, though, and I was going to gut it right there and try for another but as soon as my knife pierced its belly, a black muck oozed out, a hot, rotten smelling muck. Dead and rotten. Then there was this buzzing and a dark cloud appeared over the river. Thousands and thousands of flies, big hairy flies, and they smelled the rotten carp and swarmed in, buzzing so thick it was hard to see, and they buzzed in my ears and nose and I staggered up the bank, hardly knowing where I was going.

The air was rancid. Not just the carp, but all over the valley the air was hot and humid and rotten, and it was hard to breathe without getting sick. The closer I got to the bridge, the worse it was, and the flies were buzzing louder and all over the place, in the willows, snagged in branches, strewn across the railroad tracks, were dead pigeons, looking cynical as hell, with black muck oozing out their mouths, puddles of it, and the smell got so bad my guts churned and I was getting violently sick. One great convulsion after another. To my horror, I realized I was no longer dreaming. I really was violently sick. It was confusing as hell. I was on my hands and knees, covered with sweat and shaking.

"Food poisoning. Keep puking," I heard Caeser say into my ear. I appreciated it. I thought it was a nuclear disaster.

I lunged forward with another convulsion, smacking against the rock, then choking and everything was spinning off black and Caeser was doing a Heimlick maneuver on me, trying to pull me to my feet.

It was a terrible night. Most of the time I was delirious. Caeser helped by talking. The man could talk for hours about pigeons.

"The thing about pigeons is that they are pure. No self-ambitions. They are part of the flock, and survive as a whole."

It helped me keep my bearings. The rest of the time was spent lost, and it was terrifying to be lost.

"A solitary pigeon can't survive long on its own. A solitary pigeon is a lonely pigeon. Pigeons die of loneliness. They just give up. They draw strength from the flock. And they are the flock. They are the strength."

I woke up in the grey light of morning. I did not move for a long time. I could see out across the valley, a few early pigeons flying and a train was creeping along the tracks. My clothes were soaking wet. My head pounded, and my equilibrium was way off. It felt as though four guys had kicked me unconscious. Rising to my elbows, I tried to throw off the blankets but only lost my balance. I've never felt that bad, before or since.

"Hey Emerson, you alive?"

It was Caeser. I resented the way he said it.

"C'mon, sit up. You're gonna roll in your puke, dammit."

Caeser set me up straight and leaned against the rock. He held a jar in his hand.

"Here, you gotta try and drink some water. You're dehydrated as hell."

I didn't want any water, but he poured it down my throat, so I had to drink some. Puking cool water is a misery all its own. I felt better after a few minutes, though, and was able to keep some down. Caeser refilled the jar and set it in my hands.

"Drink as much as you can keep down. It'll cool your brain. Hell of a night, Emerson. I'm not sure Joe's going to make it."

That's when I noticed Joe lying there, about ten feet away, under a pile of blankets. Just his head stuck out, and he was in shock. His face was all drawn in and hollow, ash grey and dry. He muttered something, real low, more of a groan than anything.

"He quit puking an hour before you," Caeser said. "I think he's got more of the poison still in him."

"Weren't you sick?" I croaked, my throat raw.

"Some. Mostly just dizzy. Nothing like you two. You guys were blowing chow everywhere. It was not a pretty sight, Emerson."

I didn't want to talk about it, and to be honest, I felt so weak and miserable I didn't much care about Joe. That's hard, I know, but I just stared at him as though he was a rock.

But Caeser insisted I stay up and watch after Joe while he went for something to eat. He insisted we needed water and food, and cursed me for not caring until I nodded my head, agreeing to watch Joe.

Caeser looked like hell—thin and wore out. His eye was bloodshot, his hair stringy and greasy and hanging in his charcoal smeared face. He asked me if I had any money and I didn't, but then I remembered the two dollars Joe had taken off Murphy and Caeser went through his pockets, Joe weakly cursing him, and finally found it in the toe of his shoe. He looked in the other one and found three more. Rearranging the blankets, he tucked Joe back in, then stood and looked down at him a moment.

"Worse damn stew he ever made." Caeser said, shaking his head in bewilderment.

Caeser left and there was nothing to do but sit against the rock, drinking a little water and trying to stay awake. It was a toxic buzz, a harsh, dry sense of being crushed. My arms felt like lead, the blanket like a slab of concrete poured over my legs. Traffic crossed the bridge, rattling storm grates, the raw sound of iron crashing down with heavy blows.

Suddenly something was breathing hot and foul right in my face. My head snapped up, cracking against the rock with a burst of sparks. It was Clyde, wagging his tail in greeting. Franklin was coming up the path with Sadie. He whistled sharp, and Clyde got out of my face and went to lick Joe's ear, eliciting a groan.

"Must've been a hell of a party", Franklin joked, taking a seat in Joe's chair and watching his dogs chase the stew pot around, licking it clean and rattling it over the rocks.

Franklin had an albino squirrel in his sack and took it out to show me. It looked cynical as hell. He proudly fluffed up the pure white tail and let it flutter in the breeze.

"Found it up on Fourth Street. I'm wondering it there aren't genetic traits linked to albinism, a DNA sequence of some sort." He spoke to himself, mostly out of habit. "Sequences of recessive genes are often manifested in unison. I suspect enlarged optical cavities to enhance the light gathering capacity, increasing the ability to see in dim light. Albinos are sensitive to sunlight, you know. They haven't any natural pigment to protect themselves. Say, you know Alice? Died last night. Been sick for two days. Been eating them damn pigeons. You see all the dead pigeons laying around?"

Franklin didn't wait for me to answer.

"Of course, it just may be that the optical cavity

is smaller. I've heard of albino fish that evolved in underground pools and haven't any eyes at all. Don't need them. But a squirrel is different, I figure. A squirrel has got to be able to see, or it'd be dead meat."

He looked thoughtfully at the dead albino squirrel in his hand, smiled at his joke, then slid it back into his sack.

"Franklin," I said, "We ate pigeon stew last night. I think Joe's real sick." Franklin jumped up and chased after the yellow dog, who had won the stew pot and was carrying it triumphantly around in its mouth. Franklin grabbed the pot and brought it back to the chair, flipped it upside down, and put a foot on it. The dogs sat and cocked their heads at it.

Franklin sat scratching his head and looking at Joe. A wave of pigeons returned from the loading docks, about forty birds, arcing low and then soaring up through the bracing. A brown and white one flashed in the early sunshine, looking fresh and new, trailing the swarm of greys.

"Say Emerson," Franklin looked out at the birds, "were any of the pigeons you stewed last night brown and white?"

It made me uneasy that Franklin should ask. I almost lied about the mottled pigeon. I didn't know what he was driving at, but it was plain that Franklin had an idea, and I hesitated to confirm his hypothesis, as though his hypothesis was responsible for Joe and me getting sick. Franklin sensed my weird mood.

"Easy, son. It ain't nobody's fault. Must be a virus. Joe's just sick. No one could've known."

I told him about the mottled pigeon, peppered with brown and white feathers.

"I didn't snare it. But it fell, and Joe might've put it in the stew." Franklin was excited.

"Look, I've seen thirteen dead pigeons in the last four days. Two of them were brown and white, one laying up on seventh street, and the other down by the warehouses, the one Alice ate. Then you saw one up in the street by the Brewery. And then there's the one you ate last night. That's 21 percent of mortality by a phenotype representing no more than 3 percent of the flock. That's important statistically, Emerson. The mortality rate for brown and white pigeons may be seven times as high as it should be. A genetic link, perhaps. This could explain why brown and white pigeons are a recessive phenotype: their achilles heel, which prevents them from dominating the evolutionary process. A cyclical virus that knocks them out of the competition."

Another wave of pigeons swarmed down from the bridge, arcing low over the railroad tracks, and he watched them intently. I asked Franklin what he thought we should do about Joe, thrashing about now, trying to kick off the blankets. Franklin studied Joe.

"Alice wasn't half the size, and she must've ate four or five of the birds before it caught up with her. 'Course, Joe is old, and he might be more vulnerable. But I doubt it. Joe is as healthy as a two year old jackass. Alice ended up bleeding from both ends. Joe doing any bleeding?"

I told him I didn't think so. "Could be he's going to make it."

Franklin got up to leave, and both dogs lunged for the stew pot and he had to kick them off.

After Franklin left, I just sat there, trying to feel better. It seemed my luck had taken a dramatic turn for the worse, and I was desperate to come out of it. But there was nothing to do, just drink some water and watch Joe flop around. His thrashing was getting weaker. He looked dried out and stunned, his mouth open and face shrunken in like he'd given up. Depressing as hell. Then who comes marching into camp but Charles, another newspaper tucked up under his arm. I felt helpless. Charles had that strained, crazy look of the night before.

"You're in trouble, Emerson," he said as he seats himself in Joe's chair. There was a note of excitement in Charles' voice as he unfolded the newspaper. I started feeling worse.

"Look, your pictures' in the paper again, shaking hands with the mayor under the bridge here. Someone recognized you as the same guy he shook hands with the day before. And they reprinted the picture of you and Franklin with the mayor down by the sewer plant last May. They've run all three photos on the front page. You gave a different name each time and conflicting accounts of your dental history. It's a big scandal, Emerson. Everyone wants to know who the hell you are."

Joe let out a low groan and rolled over, flopping his face right up at Charles.

"What's wrong with him?" "He's sick."

"Sweet Jesus. I guess he's sick."

"Charles, why do people want to know who I am?"

"Because it's an election year, dammit." Charles was excited. "Someone wants to build a nuclear waste dump at the headwaters of the greatest waterway in the country, and all the bastards want to know is who the hell you are."

He looked at me, scowling with disgust.

Then Joe started kicking and the last blanket rolled off, and we could see he'd wetted himself. It was so damn depressing.

"What the hell is it?" Charles asked.

"We ate some sick pigeons, and now we're sick." Charles got this incredulous look on his face.

"You're kidding."

"The brown and white ones are especially bad for you." "Emerson, look. The next story, under you and the mayor."

He gave me the newspaper, and I couldn't help but look at the photos of the mayor, smiling with me and Franklin and the goathead and the white dog. And me and the mayor and the Dragonfly. And the newest one, under the bridge. I'm wearing my greens and a drunk, confused expression of awkwardness. It was embarrassing. The headlines read:

Mystery Man: Campaign Plant or Pathological Liar?

And the story on the bottom half of the page, in slightly less bold headlines:

Peta Protests Pigeon Poisoning Policy The city had authorized the spreading of poisoned corn around the loading docks to bring down the number of birds.

The mayor was denying any knowledge of the program. Someone was in trouble. There were dead pigeons lying everywhere. Numerous pets had taken ill after eating dead birds which had dropped into their yards. The public was outraged.

"You know what this means, Emerson?"

I said yes. I am very sick, and Joe looks like he might die.

"But not just that," he said, waving his hand as though I'd missed the point. "You're at the focal point of another controversy. The mayor is in hot water because some pigeons are dying. Imagine if a human dies, and you lying here next to him, the mystery man."

Charles looked at me in a strange way, as though bewildered at what he saw. Flabbergasted. Charles was a madman.

"The moment has come, Emerson. It's up to you. Don't ask me why. It doesn't make sense to me either. But you've been dealt the cards. Play them wisely. Soon you will be given the podium. The entire city is waiting to hear from you. Speak to them, Emerson. Tell them of the greed. Warn them of the poison, the misery we are creating. Beg them to conserve, to build windmills, solar panels, to sacrifice some small comfort for the sake of tomorrow. Help them to understand that we are responsible, and not to trust that responsibility to those who worship at the altar of greed."

Just then Caeser returned with three peaches, a half dozen bananas, and a pint of whisky.

He gave me a peach and took a shot.

"Hey, look at Joe, you clowns. Throw those blankets back over him."

Charles obeyed, piling layer after layer on Joe's twitching body. He was shivering, to be honest.

"He's got to sweat. Carries the poison out the pores. He didn't puke as much as Emerson." Caeser spoke knowingly, nodding at the job Charles had done. "He still has a lot of the poison in him. He's got to sweat it out."

Charles showed Caeser the newspaper.

"Dammit, Emerson, you're the most unphotogenic man I ever met." "Look below it," Charles was excited. "Read the story about the pigeons."

Caeser read in silence then, not making any more jokes. He stared at the paper awhile before giving it back.

"I thought there was something wrong with the flock. Damn, I should've seen that coming."

Caeser was Pigeonist Extraordinaire, Master of the Flock. The greatest damn flock in maybe the entire world. He took it personally.

"Franklin said the brown and white ones are especially bad," I said. "That make any sense to you?"

Caeser took a drink and pondered a bit. He was miserable.

"No, can't say it does. But Franklin thinks about things different.

Numbers. He studies and thinks. What did he say?" I shrugged. "Some sort of genetic link."

Charles waved the paper.

"What are you guys talking about? Genetic links, brown and white pigeons. Emerson is the focal point of the major scandal of the election. Thousands of people want to know who he is and why he's lying."

"Why?" Caeser asked.

"Because it's an election year, dammit." Charles was exasperated. "It doesn't make sense to me either. Fate? Luck? It doesn't matter. All that matters now is that he speaks out against storing nuclear waste on the river. He must make people understand how poisonous this stuff is, and that storing it on the river is a recipe for disaster. Tell them to build windmills, Emerson. Tell them to turn down their air conditioners and build smaller homes. For the sake of fairness, Emerson, teach people to accept responsibility for their actions and to begin conserving what we have."

I resented the hell out of it. I resented Charles' insinuation that I had a responsibility to enlighten the masses. None of it was my fault in the first place. And secondly, the masses don't give a damn. They don't want to know, because if they did, they'd feel guilty about it. Sure, Charles lived in a one room boxcar. He didn't have anything to worry about. But what about the poor bastard living in a four thousand square foot house with a heated garage? Those are the people who'd become victims of a guilty conscious. Charles wanted me to shatter their illusions of living in Disney Land. It wasn't my fault, and I didn't want the burden. Besides, I was messed up, just a sick bum.

A wave of pigeons swarmed down through the trusses, dropping low over the railroad tracks, then arcing upwards and heading for the loading docks. Joe groaned.

"We ate a brown and white one last night, didn't we?" Caeser asked.

I described the mottled pigeon, the way it was acting sick and how it fell.

Caeser looked down at Joe.

"Old fool, he should've seen it. It didn't even fall right. Just fell like a bag of beans, not fluttering like it was suppose to. I saw that. He should've seen it. Damn, it still had its head on, right?"

I nodded yes, but I didn't feel good about blaming Joe. He was paying the price for his own scew-up.

Charles stood up.

"Forget the damn brown and white pigeon, will you? No wonder you guys don't care about nuclear waste. You've got to learn to focus."

Charles marched off down the red rock path, newspaper tucked under his arm, shaking his head and muttering. Joe groaned and struggled weakly beneath the blankets. Caeser gave me another peach. I was starting to feel better, and thought I could stand up. I was dizzy, though, and had to lean against the rock for support. Caeser gave me a shot of whisky, and it helped steady my nerves.

"Emerson, can you think? I'm having trouble, myself. Charles is right, in a way. I can't focus. My confidence is low." He looked up at the birds flapping around on the I-beams. "My flock has been poisoned, and Joe too, and I was oblivious to it. I learned about it out of the damn newspaper, for crying out oud." Caeser sat down.

"Think of something, Emerson. I'm having trouble focusing."

It was disturbing to see Caeser so uncertain of himself. He could be irritating when he was cocky, but his melancholy was distressing. Besides, I was having trouble standing, let alone thinking.

So I ate the peach and had another shot of whisky. The peach was juicy. It was one of the best peaches I ever ate. It was their season, I guess. Nothing tastes as good as a peach in season.

Then something happened. It was almost religious. You might think I'm making it up, but I don't care. I saw it, and so did Caeser.

A white pigeon, a pure white pigeon, fluttered down from the sky and landed on the red rock. Neither of us had ever seen it before. It sat on the red rock, blinking its eyes at us, as though waiting for something. Caeser's mouth was open, my hands framed around my eyes, disbelieving. A Supreme Ludgrinian Moment. Neither of us moved. Time hung still, the bird just sitting there blinking and looking at us and us just staring back. Then the bird crapped on the rock and took off, flying down the valley. We watched it go, shining bright and clean and fresh. The only white pigeon we'd ever seen. We watched as it flew down the river, past the loading docks, and disappeared around the bend. One white pigeon flying all alone. It was almost religious. Caeser got to his feet and started cooing crazy like a madman, his arms raised, throwing his crazy pigeon call down across the railroad tracks and out over the water. Five hundred pigeons dropped from the bridge and danced over the valley, breaking and arcing and swirling, a whirlpool of birds. I swear

it all happened like that. Caeser was laughing.

"Pigeon Master!" he cried. "Caeser, Pigeonist Extraordinaire. Master of the greatest flock of pigeons in the world. C'mon Emerson, you drunk bum," he slapped me on the back, "we've got to get some help for old Joe here."

I was feeling better, too. After pausing to look at the pigeon crap on the red rock, I followed Caeser up the park path. Caeser had to stop and wait for me. He was skipping along, bouncing up the path, full of spring and bullshit. But it was steep and I was still feeling a little dizzy.

"Smile, Emerson. You live. Today is yours. The energy of the flock will sustain you."

Then he'd start cooing again, loud as hell.

The climb wore me out. I hobbled into the park leaning on Caeser, wrapped in my blanket, feeling sick and winded. The guys from the third shift parted and backed away as we approached, their conversations growing quieter. They glanced sideways at each other, but apparently none had seen the paper yet. They'd been on the line all night. They were just uneasy because we looked like hell. Except for Murphy. He thought Caeser was something special.

"I'll be damned. If it isn't the one-eyed pirate himself," Murphy bellowed, pushing through the crowd, spilling coffee. "What the hell are you doing up before noon. You got any of them eggs with you?"

Caeser started working Murphy for a cup of coffee.

"Pigeon eggs are rare this time of year, Murph, but potent. An egg produced late in the year is thick with enzymes, and if you're not careful, a man's likely to bust an artery under the wrong conditions. How's Ruth feel about it?"

"Ruth's all for it," Murphy was giggling, his big belly sticking out tight in his t-shirt. Murphy was all right. Just loud. While Caeser worked Murphy for a cup of coffee, I kind of worked my way over to Rose's station wagon, where she was serving refills and sweetrolls.

"Emerson, you look like hell," Rose said, not mean, but more like she wished I didn't. I just kind of shrugged like she'd hurt my feelings, and Rose felt bad and set me up a free cup. It steamed hot, and I appreciated it. Rose was softer than she thought.

"You bums drive me crazy."

I started shaking again. I couldn't help it and spilled some coffee on the tailgate. Rose wiped it clean, shaking her head.

"Emerson, when are you going to get away from that old bum?"

Rose looked concerned. I felt bad about working her; sneaky. To make it up, I told her about my plan to get a job at the brewery. She didn't buy it, though.

"Like hell you will. Maybe, but I won't bet on it. Maybe for six months. Then you'll say the hell with it. Your attitude is bad, Emerson. You think the world owes you, and it don't. You owe it. And you're gonna pay. But not until its shoved down your throat. Then you'll understand. But you're strong now, and free. There ain't no one going to shove nothing down your throat. Six months, tops. Ten bucks. You pay me double if you don't last a year."

Rose was so smug about it. She stood with her polishing rag, hands on her hips, daring me to take her bait. She knew it would irritate me. But suddenly it didn't. Suddenly, I felt something. A sharp, piercing sense of awareness.

Awarenss of my emotions, an understanding. My soul expanded, rising in a warm, mellow buzz, soft and easy as morning sunshine spreading across the river. Clean and honest.

Then Caeser yelled in a loud voice. "Hey Charles, c'mon over."

Charles was walking across the parking lot with a strained look about him, as though he were about to break into a run and determined not to. A newspaper was tucked up under his arm, and he carried a brown sack. Caeser yelled again. This time Charles waved, but he's not coming over.

Caeser's voice shattered the moment, the warmth fading away like the last notes of a bittersweet ballad and I closed my eyes, trying to salvage what I could to carry me for a mile, when Rose reached out and began caressing my elbow. It took me by surprise, this overt display of affection. It was out of character for Rose, which only added to its significance. Her touch was firm and electrifying, yet feminine and soothing. The intimacy of the moment was overwhelming, almost transcendental, the sense of bonding lifting me higher, and a surge of power coursed through my body. The rush, warm and peaceful, lifted me high above the mess, horizons spreading out before me like the promise of paradise.

"Rose," I said, "I love you."

Rose said nothing, but continued caressing me. Rythmically. Firm, rythmic motions. Like the shadow of a cloud, it moved across my mind.

Fool.

I opened my eyes to find Rose polishing my elbow, craning her neck in the direction Caeser was yelling. Charles was trotting across Brewery Street, dodging traffic, and disappeared into the alley heading north toward the warehouses.

"What's that?" Rose asked absently, turning to

shoo some flies off the sweetrolls, polishing her coffee maker with loving caresses. "Hey, what's the problem, Emerson? I'm serious, you look like hell."

I just kind of shrugged like none of it was worth a damn, seeking shelter in the buzz of apathy. A mess.

Caeser was laughing loud and giving Rose a hard time. "He's crazy, Rose, but he ain't no bum."

Murphy was laughing and dragging Caeser up to the tailgate to buy him a cup. Murph saw I already had a cup, so he just bought me a roll and slapped me on the back, calling me Chief Something or other because of my blanket. Caeser kept on teasing Rose.

"I wouldn't marry the crazy bastard either, Rose. Too damn serious. Naw, forget about Charles, marry me instead. How about it Rose, when are you going to marry me?"

She didn't even at him, just snorted as she poured him a cup.

"When you got enough to rent a tuxedo. Or hell freezes over, you bum." Caeser turned to Murphy.

"Sorry, Murph old buddy, but it looks like I'm going to have to raise the price of them eggs. How much they get for a tuxedo, anyways?"

Murphy got a charge out of that. Murphy got a charge out of everything. He thought Caeser was something special, though. The two of them started discussing the price of tuxedos and late season pigeon eggs and walked off. Rose finished up the refills and started polishing her coffee maker. Some of the guys are starting to leave, and there's no one by the tailgate but me. Then Rose gives me a wink, her face bright. Her eyes crinkled up, and she smiled, leaning close.

"Guess where I'm going this weekend, Emerson."

I didn't have a clue. I said Chicago, but I knew that was wrong. Some of the boxcars have Chicago Railroad painted on them. I was really messed up. Rose laughed. Rose was damn pretty when she smiled. "Yeah, right.

No, I'm going out to my sister's place in Plymouth. She called last night and invited me. She said her and the boys were going to bake me a birthday cake, and we're going to the zoo on Saturday."

Rose's eyes were shining, so that I couldn't help but smile back. "Happy birthday, Rose."

And that bastard Caeser was coming back for a refill and hears me and starts singing happy birthday to Rose in that loud, stupid voice of his, and all the guys started smiling and they start singing, and Rose tries to look tough but they're all gathered around, singing and dropping change into her tip glass and pretty soon she's got to smile, too. A tear slipped out her eye and she tried to wipe it so no one could see, and nobody lets on they do except to sing louder and smile at each other. We all walked away feeling good, Rose standing there polishing her coffee maker like she didn't give a damn about any of it.

Caeser was humming, and I was thinking everything was going to be all right, and we hadn't gone thirty yards across the parking lot when we found a dead pigeon. A grey, with its neck feathers glossy hues of purple. It looked cynical as hell. We just stood a moment, looking at the dead bird. Caeser nudged it with his foot, as though trying to wake it up.

"Damn," he said, just standing there looking at the dead bird, and it was easy to see he'd lost his focus. But a guy just gets overwhelmed by all the little pieces of bullshit so that it's hard to even worry about anything, sometimes.

"Damn. I'm tired, Emerson. Real tired."

I knew what he meant. I felt it too. But we had to start focusing. We had to get help for Joe.

We walked up to the First Street intersection, waiting for the lights to change and attracting attention. People were looking at us, judgemental as hell. My blanket was kind of loud. I never thought of it as looking really stupid before, until I stood wrapped in it on the corner of First and Brewery during the heavy morning traffic—a kind of safari thing with tigers and giraffes and zebras all over it. It was impossible to blend in. I tried acting nonchalant, casually arranging the blanket so it hung symmetrically about my shoulders. "Say, Emerson, you think they'll leave his blankets?" Caeser was staring at his feet, several toes visible out the end of his boots. Caeser didn't even have socks.

"Who?" I stared at my own feet, ashamed.

"Whoever picks up Joe. Think they'll leave his blankets? They must have plenty of blankets, don't you think? Joe's blankets ain't nothing to them, I bet they've got rooms full of blankets. Stacks of them, I bet."

I thought so. Hell, you'd think so. I told Caeser that if they did, he could have them. They were probably his at some time or other anyways.

The crowd moved, and we went with them out across the street keeping our eyes down, watching the gutter. Just as we reached the far curb, someone shoved a red 'Mckinnley for Congress' button in my hand. Caeser cursed.

"We've got to get out of here."

We'd waded right into the middle of a damn rally, neither of us paying attention. Just thirty feet up ahead the mayor was trying to give a speech and I planted my feet, trying to resist the surge of bodies pushing from behind. Yellow hardhats and lunch boxes, suitcoats and briefcases, tv cameras jockeying for position, and it was hard to even move. Roxanne Hendley, dressed sharp in red with a stunning, two tier white pearl necklace, was holding up a newspaper with my face plastered all over it, asking the mayor if he knows who I am. Ducking down, I tried to spin around and get out of there but when I turned, I found myself standing face to face with the Dragonfly. "Hello, Mystery Man," he says, smiling mean like he's got me. There was no room to run and the Dragonfly's got me by the arm. He's wearing his glasses and I could see my reflection and it was pathetic. Around the edges of his glasses his face was bruised, purple and yellow from where I'd punched him. He looked sore as hell, squeezing tighter, sneering disdainfully. Then, I swear, a dragonfly, a metalic blues dragonfly flitted in from nowhere and landed on his shoulder. It just sat there, but my mind was thick and slow and before I could think of anything to say, it was gone.

Caeser tried to step in between us, but it was too late.

"There he is!" someone yelled and the crowd pushed closer, red dots flickering on the cameras. The Dragonfly was pushing me forward and I pushed back and someone tripped and someone screamed and the reporters were sticking microphones in my face and everyone was yelling questions. I thought I was going to pass out and leaned on someone and it was the mayor, both of us caught and getting jostled around, and the traffic's all fouled up. People are trying to push through, late for work, and everyone wants to know what's going on. It's all just a blur and a rush and my head is spinning and I'm leaning on the mayor and he's trying to push me away and suddenly there's a voice booming loud over everyone else.

"Shut up and listen, dammit. Shut up, you idiots."

Caeser yelled so loud it stopped everyone in their tracks. Caeser is the craziest bastard I ever met. He's standing on the brewery steps, standing up there like a prophet, with his eye patch and scruffy beard and greasy hair flying in his face. He's got his chin jutted out and he's leaning forward, those long arms swinging loose and dangerous. He looks ready to pounce down on anyone who dared test him. He starts talking in a real ominous voice, so threatening nobody even moves. There's a crowd there now, a big crowd, and the mayor looks confused and scared. It's all out of his control.

"And who, may I ask, are you?" The mayor's trying to reinstate his authority, but Caeser doesn't budge an inch.

"I am Caeser, Master of the Flock. Pigeonist Extraordinaire. And you, sir, are a conspirator to murder if you do not listen to what I have to say."

A murmur went through the crowd and everyone's waiting for the mayor to say something, but he's as confused as everyone else.

"Under the bridge, not three blocks away, lies a victim of societal neglect. Our friend Joe lies dying, a victim of the elitist system endorsed by the Republican Party that would condemn him to a life of squalor and a death deserved by no man. He is a man, Mr Mayor, to whom you may reach out and embrace, pulling him back into the bosom of human compassion. Or whom you can ignore, as the Republicans would prefer you do, for the passing of one more unfortunate soul matters not to a soul-less system, interested only in profits and winning elections. Let the mystery man, Mr Emerson here, lead you to our friends' side. Save our friend Joe, your Honor, for though he matters not to the elitists, we love him dearly."

The mayor's face is flickering like the neon udweiser sign in Stacey's window. He wants to be a hero so bad he can hardly believe his luck, and he's so nervous about a set-up he can't make up his mind. Caeser was standing up there with his chin out, leaning forward and the crowd is dead quiet, waiting for the mayor's response. The mayor sees he's caught, and there's no way out of it.

"Mr Emerson," he says, looking into my eyes. "Lead us to your friend."

And a cheer goes up from the crowd, and everyone's moving at once and the mayor grabbed my shoulder, squeezing tight and leaning in close to my ear.

"If this is a set-up, friend, you'll be on ice by noon tomorrow." But no one else hears him because everyone's talking loud and excited and crossing the street. Horns are honking and reporters are crowding in close, asking me who the hell Caeser is, and way off in the background I can hear the crazy bastard cooing loud up on the steps, but I don't turn around because it'd be too damn embarrassing. I never saw him again.

There was no running away. I was pinned in close with the mayor, and the crowd was practically carrying us down the Brewery Street sidewalk. Traffic was at a stand still and there's an old Pontiac stationwagon and Rose is looking at me, real concerned, from behind the steering wheel. I waved at her, but she's just looking at me. I wanted to go tell her everything was okay, but the crowd was so thick there was nothing to do but keep walking down across the parking lot.

No one knew where the path was so I was shoved up ahead with the mayor and had to lead everyone down and I was thinking about poor old Joe and what a surprise this was going to be.

He was still lying wrapped in his blankets, and the mayor was afraid to get to close to him. I told the mayor it was all right, Joe was delerious but not dangerous, and there must have been fifty people coming down the path and crowding around and the cameras were rolling. I went over to Joe and kind of shook his shoulder and said, "Joe, the Mayor's here to see you," and Joe's lying there with his mouth open and for a second I thought he was already dead. But then his eyes open a little and he croaks a little. Says he wants some water.

"My God," the mayor says, "This man is dying. Give him some water."

The mayor steps in close and kneels next to Joe, kind of pushing me out of the way. He could see Joe's harmless and he's got a chance to be a hero so he's taking control.

"Get this man some water," he repeats, "And someone call an ambulance.

Dammit, someone call an ambulance NOW."

The way he says now, half a dozen people start scrambling up the path. I believe the mayor was sincere. He was certainly acting sincere about saving Joe. Of course, the cameras were running.

I had a jar of water for Joe and the mayor took it from me, and with Joe's ugly head cradled in his lap, he helps Joe take a drink, wiping his drool with his own hanky. He started giving a speech.

"This," he was saying, "is a result of Republican callousness. To allow such misery to exist is a strike against the very heart of mankind. To turn our backs on these conditions is to turn our back on compassion. It cannot be denied. The truth is laying here at your feet. Will we deny medical attention to our friend Joe here, a man to whom the basic right to health would be denied souly because he is unfortunate enough to be poverty stricken? Joe, my friend Joe, how long has it been since you've seen a dentist?"

And Joe's eyes are focused, lying there in the cradle of the mayor's lap, and he grins up at the mayor—a big, toothless, grey gummed grin, and I know he's going to be all right.

It was easy to see Joe was in good hands. The mayor wasn't going to let him die, not after a smile like that. He would've given the old bum mouth to mouth if he figured it was necessary. It would be embarrassing for him, I knew, when the fact that Joe had been pigeon poisoned was made public, but that didn't matter now.

It was time for me to disappear, being the mystery man and all. Nobody was paying attention to me, anyways. All I had to do was back off and run for the willows. The mayor was repeating his speech, about the Republicans and festering wounds, and the reporters were starting to ask questions and getting quotes. It was a good day for the mayor, and he was no longer concerned about me.

I just stood on the edge of the crowd a moment, taking the whole scene in. Just a bunch of people. I decided I liked the mayor. Sure, he was phony, but at least he was acting like he cared. I mean, he could've been acting like Joe was just worthless trash, which would've been phony, too, because the mayor was smart enough to know that everyone has potential. Maybe it's potential to help him, maybe it's potential to hurt him, but at least he understood the potential. I realized that when he whispered his threat in my ear. I mean, everyone has to act like something, so in a way, we're all phonies. I wasn't going to hold that against him. As long as he was acting worried about Joe, it was all right with me.

I turned to duck down into the willows. The sun was shining and a cool breeze was blowing and I was feeling better. Autumn was in the air, the tangy smell of yellow leaves and the river. I decided to go see Franklin. Alice meant a lot to him, and he would be feeling bad about it. I knew what I was going to tell him. That he was right. The point is, learn to enjoy the day.

But just as I turned, I caught a glimpse of someone walking down the red rock path. Walking deliberately, arms swinging straight and even, concentrating on where he was going and what he was trying to do. There was no newspaper tucked up under Charles' arm, and at first I thought that's why he appeared strange. Then I saw it. He had a gun. It's a pistol, and it's swinging with his march, pointed at the ground, like he's not enjoying carrying it at all but he's on a mission and being deliberate as hell. He's only fifty feet out and his face is resolute. He's already thought it through and it's just a matter of doing it. He looks almost calm. His eyes are big, but it's only the glasses.

Nobody see's him coming, not even the bodyguards. Joe is talking and everyone's listening to him. He's working the crowd for cigarettes. Three guys are slapping their pockets and stepping forward to give the old fox a smoke.

Even the Dragonfly is offering Joe a smoke, and the other guys aren't paying attention either. Charles is thirty feet away, swinging the gun and I knew I had to do something.

"Charles!"

But it was too late. As I ran towards him, Charles swung the gun up and fired, striking the mayor. Everyone's stunned and stood watching as Charles swings the gun back down, straight at his foot, and blows off his big toe.

The crowd came to life. The bodyguards were flying through the air, landing on Charles and ripping the gun free. Charles wasn't struggling. He went down in a limp roll, his glasses scattering across the rocks. He didn't resist at all.

I was flabbergasted. Charles was lying there, four guys sitting on top of him, and he's yelling about nuclear waste. Instincts told me to run. They were screaming, run. But I just stood there, flabbergasted at Charles. I simply could not believe the man could be so stupid.

Then I caught a glimpse of the Dragonfly. He was two seconds out and coming fast, his forearm raised and snarling and just as I turned to run, he hit, slamming us both to the ground.

It was hard to breathe. The wind was knocked out of me and the Dragonfly was twisting my arms back, and the handcuffs bit tight. He pulled me to my feet, offering me to the cameras, lights flickering red and people are yelling and pushing and someone wants to know why we did it, and Charles is yelling about nuclear waste and moral obligations. A siren's blowing, sirens everywhere, an ambulance crossing the bridge overhead, radios squawking and a helicopter circled low, the willows thrashing and whipping in the down draft.

Joe and the mayor were strapped onto some stretchers, masks taped over their mouths and someone's holding a bottle with a tube running into the mayor's arm. Joe's lying limp and he's as confused about what's going on as I am.

Two big guys pick up the mayor and head up the path, flanked by an entourage of bodyguards and cops. Two other big guys pick up Joe and begin to follow and that's when I noticed they're taking Joe's blankets. Joe was still wrapped in his blankets.

"Hey, leave the blankets, okay?" Joe looked over at me, but no one else seems to hear except the Dragonfly who tightened his grip on my arm. Everyone's talking and taking pictures, and no one seemed to give a damn.

They've got rooms full of blankets, I bet, stacked to the ceiling. They didn't need Joe's. I yelled again.

"Could you please leave the damn blankets?"

"Don't worry about it. You'll get all the damn blankets you need. Clean ones, too." The Dragonfly chuckled at his joke.

There was a hot flash of white, and a maroon wave began to lift. I became detached and thought I was going to pass out. The anger boiled dangerously, and I had to do something. The least the bastards could do is leave the damn blankets. With a sudden twist, I broke free of the Dragonfly.

"Leave the fucking blankets." I yelled, lowering my head and charging at the guys carrying Joe. They panicked and scrambled out of the way, dropping him unceremoniously to the ground.

"Emerson, you dumb bastard." Joe yelled, snaking an arm free and tearing off his mask. "Cover your ass!"

I ducked and turned just in time to catch the Dragonfly charging in on me. We collided with brain numbing impact.

He dropped like a rock.

The crowd scattered. My confidence soared.

I began charging after them like a madman, head lowered like a battering ram. Apparently, Roxanne Hendley's bright red dress attracted me, for it was her I chased down into the willows, bellering like a bull.

"Leave the fucking blankets!"

I must've hit a tree or something. I don't remember. I didn't remember any of it until the video appeared as evidence at my hearing. Embarrassing as hell.

It was, hopefully, the most humiliating period of my life. The whole city went nuts. My face was everywhere, on tv, in the newspapers. It was just pathetic. I believe it was the goatskull picture which pursuaded the judge to order my psychiatric evaluation as much as anything. He asked me what we used it for, as though Franklin and I worshipped a damn goatskull, is what he was driving at.

My lawyer insisted I'd gotten off easy, considering the DA had accused me of conspiring to murder. They were serious as hell, even though Charles swore under oath that he'd acted alone and as far as he knew, I wasn't even interested in shooting the mayor.

Angela Blackmore was gracious about the whole thing. Her smile held genuine humor as she greeted me.

"Two years, Mr Emerson, is not a long time."

Then she ordered me to put out my cigarette. Smoking was no longer allowed in the building. I did. Angela is the one who signs my release papers. She said I had to make a written request for release. That's why I wrote this. It's suppose to be theraputic. I believe it is. I feel a lot better. Stable as hell. I would like to thank the staff at Heartsfield for their insights and patience, and especially Angela Blackmore, whose administrative skills have been proven time and again to be nothing less than superlative.

Still, I must admit it has been an arduous journey.

Upon admission, I lapsed into an extended period of sulking. I felt victimized by the system. No one seemed to notice much, since they were all used to my apathy anyways. There's not much difference in outward appearance between a guy who's sulking and one who's just apathetic. They're both idiots and neither tends to talk much. It was a hell of a fix, though, because I knew, this time, that as far as a menace goes, I was a phony. Yet everyone thought of me as more of a menace than ever, when all I was really doing was sulking because I was a victim. I glorified in my victim status and sulked around Heartsfield, misunderstood, for eight months. I figured the system had really dealt me a losing hand this time.

The reason I snapped out of my sulking mode was because Charles' lawyer pleaded him insane, and he was committed to Heartsfield eight months after I was. I could not act like a victim around Charles.

He got off light because he's a crazy bastard, and he was insulted as hell about it. He showed up with a limp, wild eyed ranting and the first thing he did was form a committee, Morons Against Nuclear Waste or something. Ron joined the committee, and Charles made him vice chairman. Every

Wednesday they hold a meeting in the rec room, and the tv is turned off for two hours while they discuss the hazards of nuclear waste.

Charles was furious because the mayor had been elected to the Senate on a landslide. The papers portrayed the mayor as a martyr, even though Charles had only nipped him in the ass cheek with a .22 caliber short load. The whole business had backfired on Charles. The fact that he'd shot himself in the foot out of empathy for the mayor was lost in the newspaper. He was seen simply as an incompetent madman.

Charles was mad, but I believe he'd put the bullets exactly where he wanted them. Caeser was right, in a way. Charles really was a pacifist. He just got caught up in a moment.

To make matters worse, Joe helped get the mayor elected. He became some-thing like the mayor's poster child. He appeared in a series of campaign adds. First, they showed him cradled in the mayor's lap; a drooling, dirty and miserable mess. Then, in the next picture, he's got on a new suit and he's clean and well fed and happy looking, smiling with a full set of dentures so that it didn't even look like the same man. And he's telling us how good a guy the mayor is and what a difference nice teeth have made in his life. Then the mayor steps in and puts an arm around Joe, and they look at each other and smile and the picture fades.

I was sitting in the rec room the first time the add ran, and I thought Charles was going to bust an artery.

"Emerson!" He jumped to his feet, shaking a newspaper at the tv screen, his eyes wild. "Can you believe this charade? My God, that's not even Joe. He's been brainwashed. They've probably got him on prozac, for Christ's sake."

Actually, I was kind of proud of the old fox. Joe was the sneakiest man I've ever met. He never told anyone that he'd eaten poisoned pigeons. Come to think about it, he probably never knew. Or cared. Neither did anyone else. No one gives a damn about a bunch of pigeons, anyways. Unless they're causing property damage.

As hard as it was for me to believe I was in a mental institution with Charles, what really got me was that two weeks after he was committed, Rose came to visit him. And now she stops in every Sunday afternoon with a box of cookies she's baked for the crazy bastard.

And I've got to sit here and listen to them discuss the implications of storing nuclear waste on the greatest waterway in the nation as though they were meant for each other. Sometimes they start giggling, for Christ's sake. Charles giggling. It was pathetic.

I'm still a little disappointed in Rose.

Franklin died that winter. He froze to death in his tunnel. It was a brutal winter, just like he predicted. The reason I heard about it was because his dogs were scavengers and survived by feeding on Franklin himself. They were good dogs, despite the way the newspapers told the story. I guess it doesn't really matter, but it was still irritating. Perhaps, as Franklin was portrayed, he was insane; a misfit who collected animal skulls and lived in a sewer tunnel. Maybe so, but there was a lot more to it than that.

Murphy said he heard Caeser was in jail in South Dakota for cattle rustling. It's probably not true, though.

Printed in the USA
CPSIA information can be obtained
at www.ICGtesting.com
BVHW041957300723
667948BV00011B/50